The Unraveling Of Fate

A NOVEL BY C. R. C.

Disclaimer:
This is a work of fiction. All characters, locations, and businesses are purely products of the author's imagination and are entirely fictitious. Any resemblance to actual people, living or dead, or to businesses, places, or events is completely coincidental.

"Not even in death will our souls be parted. We will find one another again and begin anew. Our love is eternal and unwavering, like the tides of the sea. I will meet you there." -E

Chapter 1

Two paths have now become one, just as fate intended. Making heartfelt decisions has never been Rose's strong suit, but the time has come nonetheless to make a formal decision.

Should she reconcile with Phillip? Or should she choose to create a new future with Emery?

Being stuck at a crossroads would drive anyone mad when the battle between the heart and mind rages on. Many advise to listen to one's heart; perhaps it won't make sense, but it will more than likely feel right.

As Emery sits across the table from Rose in the charming little restaurant in Carmel, her attraction to him is palpable. She is nervous, and her hands are cold. She bundles them in the cashmere scarf on her lap, almost wishing she wasn't sitting here at all.

Simply put, Rose can't handle the intensity between them. Much like a loaded gun waiting to go off, the passion that they lived through together all those lifetimes ago makes their present moments far more intense. In any case, Rose figured that maybe if she didn't choose, she could possibly be let off the hook altogether. But then again, not choosing was still in fact choosing, in a way.

Her heart draws her to Emery like a magnet; she can't deny that. She fears losing control with Emery, of letting herself go and surrendering to this love fate has delivered to her.

Emery, on the other hand, is much better at keeping his feelings under wraps; his cool composure hides the simmering lust and love he feels for Rose. Such thoughts haunt him throughout his day, making it difficult to focus on much of anything else.

Emery also can't deny that while he doesn't want to rush things with Rose and possibly scare her off again, a more primal part of him *wants* to rush. He wants to take her and relive their intimate moments, the pleasure lingering afterwards for hours, like a high from ecstasy that only they can give one another.

But their intimate moments together are more than just pleasurable, they are healing, too.

Yet, if they're not careful, their carnal lust for one another could potentially turn obsessive. Like an addict craving their next fix, when the love withdrawals start to set in, things could turn dark very quickly.

More than anything, Emery is terrified of losing control again like he did in the past, in a fit of jealous rage. His emotions took control and landed him in a place there was no coming back from, the karmic repercussions too great to shoulder.

Because he knows what he is capable of—it scares him, and it is not something he wishes to repeat… but for Rose, there is no telling what he would do.

It is quiet at their table as they look at each other, both hypnotized as if the world around them has stopped. The energy between them is charged; without needing to say much they have a quiet moment before the waiter comes over with their food.

As the man places Rose's plate in front of her, she is snapped out of her trance-like state.

Emery shifts over the napkin in front of him to accommodate his plate. "Thank you," he says to the waiter with a nod.

Before he leaves, the waiter refills both of their wine glasses.

Rose watches the candlelight on their table as it reflects off the drinks, biting her lip. Emery smiles at her, trying to find the right thing to say.

Finally, Rose turns her gaze back to him. "This place is nice, isn't it?"

He raises his brows, happy she started the conversation between them. "Yes, it is!" he replies, chuckling slightly.

"So," Rose says, digging a fork into her meal, "what is your life like back home? Are there similarities to your past incarnation?"

Emery smirks and takes a sip of wine. "Yes, it is quite fascinating. It's almost as if they just copied and pasted the past into this life."

"How so?" Rose presses, glancing up.

"Well, for one would be my family. Same setup. My parents, the same as it was in the past. Except I don't have a brother in this lifetime. It's just me, which is unfortunate because I would've loved to give up all the pressure placed on me and relinquish it to a sibling so I could be free," he confesses with a laugh.

"Pressure?" Rose quirks a brow.

Emery nods, eating a bite of his meal. "Yes, since I am the only heir to my family's fortune, I've been preparing since I was born to take over for my father when he's ready to retire, and let's just say I don't exactly like the cards that have been dealt to me. It's not my cup of tea to run the family business, if you know what I mean."

Rose watches Emery attentively as he speaks.

"I'm not as free I'd like to be back home," he continues. "It's not like it is here, with you. No one knows me here in Carmel, and I love that. My father expects me to marry and live in England. Raise my children and grow old there. The empire my family has built is most important to him, and I understand the pressure he is under. But I just don't want to be tied down there; it's not a peaceful place for me."

Emery takes a sip of his wine and steers the topic to Rose. "What about you?" he asks. "Any similarities?"

"Yes," she answers with a slight nod. "But not too many things, family wise. It is more in the love department, I would say. Only, it's flipped; I married Phillip instead of you this time around."

Emery's body stiffens and becomes unsettled when Rose mentions Phillip. His heartrate begins to speed up. "May I ask how you feel about all this?" He wants to get inside Rose's mind, he is so eager to know what she thinks. Rose can see in his face that he's unsettled at the mere thought of Phillip still being in the picture.

"I felt very scared upon initially finding out all this," she admits, making a face. "I think I sensed it coming, sort of like a premonition. But I wasn't too sure what it would be. When I first saw you, it really hit me that the regressions were not a lie or some hallucination." Rose swallows over the lump in her throat and nervously drinks from her glass to soothe the uneasy feeling brewing inside her. "That was hard to grasp."

"I was very skeptical, for a while," Rose continues. "But something kept drawing me back; I couldn't leave it alone. I had to know the truth—I wanted to know more. And then in one of the sessions, I felt you. In the other regressions, I could get a sense of what was going on and how I felt, but in that memory..."

She pauses, looking down at the table and recalling what she had seen.

"We were standing in your family estate's garden with the white roses your mother loved so much. You hugged me and made me feel safe." Rose toys with her necklace a bit, a soft smile playing on her lips. "The energy lingered for a while after. I couldn't quite shake it, and I found myself missing you without having even met you in this lifetime yet!" She can't help but blush now. "It is the most interesting thing to experience."

Emery watches her, hanging on to her every word. "You know, my mother has a beautiful rose garden. All white roses, too," he says softly.

"Just like in the past incarnation?" Rose asks, bewildered.

"Yes. Just like in the past. She loves white roses. That garden is her baby. Maybe I'll take you soon to see it," Emery says, a wistful smile spreading on his face.

Rose balks at him. "Really? You don't think it's too sudden?"

"Of course not. Besides, I should tell you; my mother is a psychic intuitive. She knows about you already, but she was very vague with me on information." He waves her off, taking a bite of food.

"So, I bet she saw me coming," Rose muses.

Emery nods, raising a shoulder in a shrug. "More or less."

After dinner, they leave the restaurant and head to Emery's home. They drive past Rose's address, where she now resides alone for the time being. Phillip has moved to another neighborhood nearby. Although separated, nothing is formally drafted yet.

Phillip hopes to win Rose back, of course. She knows he won't give up, and she ponders whether she should give their marriage another chance, but she can't help herself from wanting to explore Emery.

At the very least, the alcohol in her system is helping keep the nerves at bay. Instead of driving Rose home, Emery decides to drive to his place first and once there, give her the option to end their evening together or spend more time with him. He can only hope she gifts him a little more time.

Emery drives the car into his garage before easing to a stop, and Rose opens her door and tries to get out, forgetting she still has her seat belt on. Emery begins to laugh, leaning over to click her seatbelt and release her. "Thanks," Rose answers, her cheeks flushed pink from embarrassment.

Emery walks over to her side of the vehicle and takes her by the hand, assisting her in getting out. "Would you like me to walk you home?" he asks.

"Do you want to call it a night?" Rose retorts, brows pinched in confusion.

"No, no. I just don't want to assume," Emery says nervously.

Rose smiles and nods. With her hand in his, Emery leads her into his home. They sit by the fireplace in his living room and talk a bit more, picking up where they left off. Feeling a little daring, Emery decides to bring up some passionate moments from their shared past.

"Did you see them, too?" Emery asks Rose, voice husky.

Her desire for him rises as he speaks in such a straightforward manner.

She looks into his eyes as she recalls the memories in her mind's eye. She blinks, slightly flustered, as she becomes aroused.

Emery leans in slowly, her perfume drifting in his direction seductively pulling him in. His nose gently presses against hers as his mouth descends upon her lips, stopping just before reaching; the sexual tension between them is electric.

Rose can't take his teasing anymore and kisses him,

unleashing the lust within each of them. In that moment, it appears to her as though Emery receives the permission he was seeking.

His hands glide up Rose's dress, and she lets out an impassioned gasp as his fingers gently stroke her clitoris. Her hands grip his shoulders, and she closes her eyes.

The pleasure from his touch is overwhelming, unlike anything she has ever felt in her lifetime. As she moans, melting under Emery's caresses, Emery undoes the zipper of his pants to relieve his erect penis. He devours Rose with every kiss as if it were his last. Rose's body trembles with delight.

"Let's move to the room," Emery whispers in her ear as he kisses her neck.

She nods, completely subjugated by him. He lifts her in his arms and carries her to his bedroom. Closing the door behind him, he hastily places Rose on his bed. It's a moment he has been craving for a long time.

Rose undresses him, eager to continue. She has never felt such lust; his essence is intoxicating. Emery rests on top of her as he stimulates her further.

His lips kiss hers gently, and he works his way down to her clitoris to finish what he started, pausing every few seconds to savor her taste.

Enjoying her moaning pleas to continue, he gently presses the tip of his penis in, watching as it enters her ever so delicately. Emery peers up at Rose, taking in the glorious sight of her flushed cheeks and bare breasts before him.

"Please," she begs through panting breaths.

Emery kisses her lips once more, thrusting all the way in and eliciting a gasp from Rose. With every thrust, the energy builds and builds, and just before she is about to come, he slows down to withhold it for a second more.

Emery looks into Rose's eyes and kisses her as they climax together. Completely drunk from pleasure, they entangle their naked bodies as close as possible. They gaze into one another's eyes and in that moment, Rose makes her choice.

"I want you," she breathes.

His blue eyes light up with tender dedication, this delicate moment now forever impressed in his psyche. Her voice still a little breathless from their moment together, he relishes the words he has been wanting to hear since he first saw her again.

"Are you sure?" Emery presses, thinking she might've wanted more time.

Rose kisses him passionately before answering, "Yes, I'm sure."

Chapter 2

Emery begins to fall asleep while closely snuggling Rose in his arms. She admires him as his eyes drift closed. Being with him again feels right, as if she is right where she is meant to be.

Truthfully, she didn't think she was going to blurt out her choice so soon, but it became apparent that her rightful place in life is with him. Everything seemed to click; in his embrace, Rose felt safe enough to take a leap of faith despite her fears. Now fast asleep, Rose kisses Emery, his once restless mind at peace.

The woman he desired desperately after all this time is completely secured in his arms.

But bringing Rose and Emery together is just the beginning of what fate has in store.

Their love isn't meant to be easy, not in the slightest. No love ever is, no matter how destined.

They will be tested. The obstacles thrown their way will be no mere coincidence. But it is up to them both to either draw closer together or let these challenges tear them apart.

Rose gets up from Emery's bed and looks through his closet for a coat to wear out at the beach. It's late, about 2 a.m. After getting dressed, she quietly let's herself out of his home and walks across the street to the beach per usual. It is her favorite thing to do, hearing and seeing the waves crash on the beach. The delightful sound of the ocean invigorates Rose.

Wearing nothing but Emery's large ankle-length coat, her bare feet make their way down the sandy staircase. At the last step, she leaps onto the cold, soft sand. The misty air delights her senses. Rose plops down on the sand gleefully as Emery's scent lingers on her skin.

Back in his bed after only five minutes, Emery awakes to see Rose is missing beside him. He jolts up and throws on some clothes to search for her.

After walking swiftly around the house and failing to find her, Emery notices Rose left her phone on the sofa in the living room. He walks out his front door and looks around. Seeing a feminine silhouette out on the beach, he runs there to investigate.

Rose turns to look to Emery's house and sees someone approaching. She smiles; he must've woken up upon not feeling her close to him.

As he arrives, she pops open his coat, playfully showcasing her naked body in the moonlight.

"Oh my god!" Emery blurts out over the sound of the waves.

"I hope you don't mind that I borrowed your coat," Rose quips with a giggle.

Emery's eyes go wide. A tiny smirk forms on his face as she walks over to rest in his arms.

"Why didn't you wake me? I would've come with you," Emery scolds, kissing her temple. Rose shrugs as they walk together down the beach.

"I don't know, you were asleep. I didn't want to wake you."

Emery sighs, running a hand through his dark hair. "Wake

me next time. I don't want you out here alone. And naked?" He side-eyes her and shakes his head with a smirk. "Not on my watch."

Rose runs off without warning into the waves, playfully sweeping up to her feet. The coat on her body opens slightly, revealing her bare breast.

Emery smiles as he watches Rose play in the water. He is over the moon to be in her presence; it was utter torture for him to be so close to Rose yet so far with the barriers in place. Now that Rose has made her choice, he has thoughts of planning a trip back home. He wants to take her with him and introduce her to his parents.

Emery has big plans for their future. Rose is the woman he wants to marry and have children with. He won't wait long to propose, as he feels a real sense of urgency to cement things; he fears that Phillip may want to work his way back into her life.

Selfishly and possibly cowardly, he can't help but feel a little insecure. What if Rose were to change her mind? It would destroy him, and he can't have that.

Emery wants Rose for himself at any cost. He knows it isn't the most perfect of thoughts.

But nonetheless, he can't help himself.

He goes to join Rose in the water but instantly shudders. "Oh my God! This is freezing!" he blurts out, making Rose laugh.

"It's not that bad!" she argues, splashing him.

"You're insane! No way," Emery cries, hurrying back to the safety of the sand. Rose chases after him, still laughing.

"Baby!" she shouts.

Rose hugs Emery, clinging to his body as she kisses his neck. Looking up into his eyes, she wishes she could freeze this moment forever.

"Fate is a wild thing, isn't it?" Rose whispers breathlessly.

11

His eyes longingly peer into hers. "I want you forever," he whispers back. "With every breath I take and exhale, I want you now and in the next life."

Rose kisses Emery back as they stand on the beach under the moonlight in each other's embrace. His body fervently aches with desire; she is everything he ever dreamed of and more.

"Do you understand?" he says with his hands gently resting on the sides of her neck and face. "I mean that. With all that I am. I want you forever."

Rose melts listening to Emery, utterly breathless. She nods.

"Let's go inside and you can show me how much you want me," Rose responds seductively.

Emery beams and follows her inside.

As soon as Rose steps foot in the house, she drops Emery's coat at her feet, but before she can make a break for the bedroom, Emery quickly wraps his arms around her naked body, preventing her from getting away.

His hands gripping her hips firmly, Emery gradually drops to his knees before Rose. He begins to kiss her thighs with utter tenderness, his hunger insatiable. Following his instincts, Emery takes Rose in his arms and moves in front of the fireplace, his body trembling as he struggles to pace himself.

"The window is open. Someone could see," Rose says, her voice barely above a whisper.

Emery grins. "If you want, we can turn the fireplace on so they can have a better look."

"Okay," Rose says jokingly.

Emery proceeds to turn on the fireplace.

"I wasn't serious!" Rose retorts, gaping at him.

He merely smirks and plants a kiss on her lips. "No one is going to see. Besides, it's late. No one gets up at this hour," Emery whispers.

Rose raises a brow at him, trying not to laugh. "You're a freak."

"What?" Emery snorts, leveling her with a serious look.

Rose kisses him and positions herself atop his body, her long dark hair disheveled.

As their eyes meet, they are both drawn closer to each other. Their souls feel as if they're merging into one.

Rose rests her body on Emery's, her breasts pressing against his chest. His hands roam freely over her soft body. Rose reaches for Emery's large, erect penis and frenziedly guides him into her.

Rose can't help but close her eyes; the pleasure is almost too much for her to take.

Emery desperately flips Rose beneath him. She can sense her moaning is arousing Emery further as his thrusts become deeper and harder. He has grown to like controlling Rose's orgasms. He prolongs them for a long as he can.

Part of Rose secretly hates that he has this power over her. But she couldn't run away even if she wanted to. The pleasure afterwards leaves her body trembling. The euphoria lingers for hours. The way Emery makes love to her feels as if their breathing is almost synchronized.

An unexpected tear rolls out of the outer corner of her eye as she finishes. Rose moans breathlessly, tightly closing her eyes as she relishes the pleasure radiating all over her body. Emery's kisses intensify the sensation by a thousand-fold.

He lays beside Rose as he finishes right along with her.

Both gasping and at a loss for words, they lay there in disbelief at how pleasurable the sex was, almost torturous even.

"We can't be away from each other," Emery asserts, shaking his head in awe. "We just can't. Not after this."

A little disoriented, Rose snuggles up to him, embracing

his warmth. "I think you're right," she agrees, still trying to catch her breath.

"This is insane," Emery confesses, chest still heaving from the exertion of what they'd done. "What are you made of?"

Rose shakes her head and smirks at him. "It was so intense my eye shed a tear."

Emery turns to her abruptly, brow creased in concern. "I thought so!"

"I have never felt anything like this before in my life. I swear to you," she declares trying to make sense of it all.

"I'm right there with you." Emery smiles softly.

Rose kisses Emery before resting her head on his chest and finally dozing off.

"One lifetime is never enough," he whispers to Rose, unaware that she has fallen asleep.

Emery kisses her soft hand that lays on his chest; he can almost picture an engagement ring on her ring finger.

It can't be just any stone, he thinks to himself. *It must be special and unique like their love.*

The large emerald cut ring he had given her in their past life comes to mind. What a wonder it would be if he could find it. Emery is hopelessly, madly in love with Rose; he is eager for his mother to meet her.

He knows she will be smitten. His father too, although Emery knows his father will begin to pressure him to come back home and settle in England for good.

His heart sinks in his chest a little at the thought. When he envisions his future with Rose, he sees them living in Carmel, away from all the noise and constant harassment of the family business.

Above all, Emery fears Rose leaving him when she realizes what being with him entails back home. He hugs a fast-asleep

Rose a little tighter in his arms, hoping their love is strong enough to endure what may come. He can't imagine losing her, and he refuses to live without her.

If he must renounce his obligations in his family, then so be it. He would give it all up for her. All these thoughts render Emery a restless night.

For the moment, he forces himself to relish every serene moment with Rose in their own little bubble. Because once they arrive in England, they won't have much peace and quiet for a while. Ever so softly, Emery lifts a sleeping Rose in his arms and carries her away to his bedroom, determined to take on their future together.

Chapter 3

The following morning, Emery wakes up to the smell of coffee wafting into his room. He can hear his latte machine's steamer clearly from where he lays in bed.

Throwing on the nearest bottoms he can find, he rushes over to the kitchen where he knows Rose is. His heart flutters in his chest with excitement; he is a complete fool in love, and he is not ashamed to admit it in the slightest.

Emery hurries out of his bedroom and into the hallway where a slowly moving Rose stands with two large latte cups filled to the brim with morning brew.

"I was going to surprise you." Rose mutters in disappointment.

Emery grins and takes a cup from her. "The machine is loud. It woke me."

"Well, anyway. I hope you like it. I even made a little heart at the top for you." She nods towards the frothy decoration.

"I still haven't attempted latte art. You'll have to show me how you did that," Emery says, visibly impressed. "Shall we sit in the living room?"

Rose nods and turns around slowly, trying not to spill her coffee on Emery's floors.

He rests his hand on her waist, unaware of his effect on her.

"Don't do that," Rose says breathily.

"What?" Emery asks, brows pinched in confusion.

"I'm telling you; your touch alone is enough to make me feel out of control. It is very arousing. I can't control it," Rose confesses, her cheeks flushing. "Even just the thought of you. Is stimulating enough."

Emery laughs, pleased. "I am very happy it is mutual," he says after taking a sip of his coffee.

They sit in the living room and stare at one another, completely infatuated.

"Will you come with me back home? Just for three weeks maybe?" Emery suggests.

Rose raises her brows. "You don't think it's too soon to meet your parents, do you? Won't they be alarmed?" she asks.

Emery shakes his head. "No, not at all. Won't you come?"

She sighs looking down at her steaming mug. "I'm kind of scared. What if your family doesn't like me?" she murmurs.

"Stop," Emery immediately cuts off that line of thought. "It's not my parents you have to worry about. It's family friends, more likely."

"What?!" Her head snaps up to stare at him. "No, I'm not going."

"Come on, I'll protect you," Emery assures her whilst rubbing her leg affectionately.

She scrunches her nose, unconvinced, but shrugs. "When do we leave?" she inquires.

"How about tonight?" Emery suggests "We can sleep on the plane and rest at my parents. The house is more than accommodating and private, very private."

"I'll have to pack quickly then," Rose sighs, making a mental checklist.

"Alright." Emery nods and promptly gets up to make the

arrangements to have the family jet ready for that night. "My mother will be very excited to have us."

Rose gives Emery an uneasy nod. She can't help but be a little nervous. It's his mother, after all. And what if it's too soon? They've only just met, and already he wants her to meet his family.

Rose ponders whether she should come up with an excuse to not meet them just yet. Emery will most likely see right through her, and her attempt at evading this situation would be futile.

Resigned to the situation, she finishes her cup of coffee and lets Emery know she is heading over to her place down the street to pack. Emery is on the phone with the staff at the airport and simply nods in acknowledgement at Rose.

About an hour after Rose enters her home she used to share with Phillip, she hears a knock at her front door.

"It must be Emery," she thinks aloud to herself. She throws a few things into her luggage and runs downstairs. But when she opens the front door, she's startled to see Phillip standing before her.

"Are you okay?" Phillip asks, noticing her uneasy expression.

"Uh, yes." She swallows. "Hi. What, what are you doing here?"

Phillip's hand trembles as he struggles to maintain eye contact. "I wanted to see you."

Rose hears his words but is terrified of what might happen if Emery were to show up, if Phillip knew she had moved on and officially made her choice. She is not ready to tell him yet. He would be devastated.

Rose's feelings towards the end of their marriage are complex. Something she struggles to comprehend. She sees now that Emery is her future; they are simply meant to be. It is obvious to her now. But she also knows Phillip most likely won't take the news very well.

"Oh," Rose says awkwardly. "I'm terribly busy right now, so I can't talk much. Maybe another time?" She forces a smile.

"Really?" Phillip says, frowning in disappointment.

Rose nods, merely offering a shrug in return.

They stand there at the front door, now gazing at each other as if strangers to one another.

"I love you," Phillip confesses whole-heartedly. "I want you. I want another chance."

Rose's eyes grow wide. She stands there at her front door, frozen by Phillip's confession.

"Please say something," Phillip pleads when her silence becomes suffocating. He doesn't understand why Rose has a petrified expression on her face. He turns to follow her gaze behind him.

Emery's piercing blue eyes glare through Phillip's core. His typical cool and collected demeanor fades to reveal his simmering jealousy coming to the surface.

Rose stands there looking at both Phillip and Emery, mortified. *This can't be happening*, she thinks to herself. Her heart races in her chest; she must think of something quickly. But Emery beats her to it.

"Hi," Emery begins in a very cold tone.

Phillip spins around, surprised to see his neighbor behind him. "Oh, can we help you with something?" he asks, completely oblivious as to why Emery might be here.

Emery raises a brow at Phillip. If looks could kill, Phillip would be dead.

"I'm here to see Rose," he answers smoothly, walking past Phillip and up to Rose.

Emery stands beside her and takes her hand.

It's then that Philip finally realizes what has happened. His brows furrow, and an irate expression forms on his face.

"Oh, really?" he seethes, his lips curled in disgust.

Emery smirks. "Yes, really."

Phillip turns his glare to Rose. "We need to talk," he says to her.

As Rose is about to speak, Emery cuts in. "I don't think you have much to talk about anymore," Emery says, gripping Rose's hand tighter as he attempts to move her body behind him.

"Emery," Rose whispers. "Stop."

Emery ignores Rose and continues to stand his ground against Phillip, pushing him away. This only earns him a shove back in response, a challenge.

"She is still my wife!" Phillip shouts. "Stay the fuck out of this!" He spins to face Rose, eyes narrowed. "We need to talk."

Emery steps out in front of Rose. "I think it's over," he snarls.

Phillip shoves Emery back. "I was talking to *her*."

Rose steps in-between them. "Stop, both of you." she says, visibly shaken. "Don't do this." She glances across the street to where people are walking by, then up at Emery. "Please."

Phillip grabs Rose's hand, Emery's eyes widen. His volcanic emotions that were so carefully restricted, finally erupt. "Don't fucking touch her," Emery sneers with a clenched jaw.

Phillip loses it and punches Emery as hard as he can. Landing a blow to his lip, he sends Emery flying back a step. He takes hold of the door behind him to steady himself.

Phillip shouts, "She's my wife, you piece of shit! Aren't you bold?"

Rose gasps and steps away from both men.

Emery wipes the blood off his lip and punches Phillip back with an enraged snarl.

"Stop!" Rose shouts helplessly. "Stop!"

She can't believe her eyes. Both Emery and Phillip have at it releasing their anger upon each other with blows. Rose feared for good reason telling Phillip the news, but she didn't want him to find out this way. *Emery instigated the situation*, she thinks to herself, now angry at both Emery and Phillip and their sheer stupidity. Rose goes inside and leaves them out there to quarrel on their own.

After a minute or two, Phillip finally backs away from Emery.

"This isn't over," he seethes, wiping blood from his nose. He nods toward the house behind him, where he can see Rose through the window. "You think she will want anything to do with you now?" he says with a smirk, showcasing blood on his teeth.

Emery catches his breath and looks behind him to see Rose visibly shaken, staring at him.

"You can't control your temper. There is something to be said about your display here. I may be on the outs, but I think you are too, now," Phillip says, raising a brow. "That jealousy and rage are dangerous to display so early in a relationship. Everyone knows that."

Emery glares at Phillip, clenching his fists at his sides.

"I wouldn't be surprised if she withdraws from you," Phillip taunts with a smile in Emery's direction. "Good luck."

Emery watches as Phillip gets in his car to leave. Once he drives off, Emery stands there for a few seconds and looks down at his feet, afraid he might be right.

Chapter 4

Rose goes up to her bedroom and locks the door behind her. Completely shaken by the confrontation outside, she retreats into herself and remembers what the guides said to her during her past life regressions with Catherine.

The past must not repeat itself. Yet here they all are, repeating the same behaviors that occurred in the past. Rose is worried Emery won't be able to evolve past his jealousy and intensity. Passionate love is one thing, but when taken too far, it can become toxic.

Rose sits on the floor in front of her bed, almost emotionless as her mind continues to race.

Emery knocks at her bedroom door. He tries to turn the knob, but the door is locked.

"Rose," he calls out from the hall.

Rose can't find the motivation to let him in.

"Rose," Emery tries again, voice pleading.

She doesn't answer, instead preferring to keep to herself for a while. She will talk to him when she's ready.

After an hour, Rose leaves her bedroom and heads downstairs into her kitchen for a drink of water. The house is quiet, and she assumes Emery must've left to his own home. But as she enters the kitchen, she sees Emery sitting in her living room.

As soon as he sees her, Emery walks over. "Rose," he begins.

A stoic Rose grabs a cup and fills it with water, refusing to look at him.

"I'm sorry," Emery says to her. Standing beside her, he slowly reaches for her arm.

Rose puts her water down after drinking a bit and lets out a disappointed sigh.

"Did the guides also tell you that the past must not be repeated?" Rose asks.

Emery's eyes peer at Rose. "Yes," he says, his tone filled with shame.

"If you can't break the cycle of your behavior, we have no chance," Rose snaps, stalking away from Emery toward the living room, where she sits on the couch.

"I know I messed up," Emery answers, averting his gaze. "I just... it's difficult for me to control my emotions. They're intense. I love you so deeply that the thought of losing you drives me mad."

Rose refuses to look at Emery as he speaks, making him go over to her to plead his case.

"I will do my best to control myself. I will try, but Phillip knew what he was doing, too. It isn't just me. He tries to get under my skin," Emery insists.

Something clicks in Emery; he looks up, astonished.

"Just like he would do in the past," Emery recalls.

"What?" Rose asks, unsure of what he means.

"He would try to get under my skin by pushing boundaries; he would get close to you." He shakes his head. "At the ball, when he invited you over to see his home through his friend. He planned it. It doesn't excuse what I did, obviously. But we are locked in this karmic cycle, all three of us."

"Yup," Rose says. Nodding solemnly.

"How do we break it?" Emery wonders.

Rose stares at him. "Stop doing the behaviors you did in the past. "Pretty simple. Not easy, but simple."

Emery shakes his head, annoyed. "Well, he better stay the fuck away from you," he mutters.

Rose takes his trembling hand and squeezes it tightly. "Stop," she whispers.

It is utter torture for Emery—the feelings that arise within him. He is utterly infatuated with Rose; it is compulsive. The passion he feels for her is intoxicating.

He struggles to keep himself on an even keel. These emotions are his karmic repercussions for his past actions. He struggles more than Rose, that much is obvious.

"I must get myself under control. I can't lose you," Emery professes faintly, letting out a sigh. Rose can hear the struggle in his tone. "It would be the end of me."

He turns his intense oceanic gaze towards Rose, his vulnerability on full display.

Rose moves closer to Emery and kisses him.

"I'm yours," she attempts to assure him, but even she has a sliver of doubt. This love is dangerous if they cannot tame the darker impulses lurking within their connection.

Emery kisses her back with urgency. Rose climbs onto Emery's lap and proceeds to pull off his shirt. Emery's hands swiftly find their way under Rose's dress. He removes her underwear while Rose unfastens his jeans.

As Emery penetrates Rose, both intently gaze into one another's eyes.

The reassurance Emery was quietly seeking from Rose, he finds loudly in her moans. She has a power over him he can't quite put into words; sex with her is fervent and all-consuming.

How could Emery possibly doubt Rose's devotion to him

when she gives herself over to him so completely? Their love isn't perfect, it is dangerously deep and complex. But it is theirs all the same.

As they come together, intense pleasure pulses through their bodies. Two souls becoming one, deeply intertwined in one another.

Their intimate connection is no ordinary connection; their joint orgasms are tantric and supernatural. Although uneasy about Emery's intense emotions, the sexual connection is so intoxicating, Rose can't turn away from it. She is ensnared by the pleasure Emery brings her.

❧❦❧

Emery firmly grips Rose close. His lips delightfully press themselves on her neck, completely drunk off her floral scent.

"We have to get going soon," Emery regretfully whispers, wishing this moment could last longer.

"What?" Rose says, coming back to reality from their lustful haze.

"Our trip," Emery answers, reminding her of the arrangements he had made earlier.

"Oh," Rose murmurs. "I don't know."

Emery avoids eye contact with Rose and sulks. "Please?" he asks. "It will be fine."

Rose shrugs and gets up to grab her luggage. "Fine!" she mutters, giving in.

A delighted smile forms on his face as soon as she agrees. Emery gleefully trails behind her.

He is on cloud nine that Rose is coming with him, even more so after what occurred with Phillip. He can't let Phillip have the chance to come around her again. Emery hatches a plan to keep him at bay, although he suspects she might be on to him.

Chapter 5

They arrive at the airport that night to board Emery's family jet. It is the first time Rose has ever boarded a private plane, and she's in awe of the luxury before her. She heads up the stairs to be greeted by Sophie, the flight attendant Emery had flown with when he first arrived.

"Hi!" she says to Rose politely and shows her to her seat. "Nice to see you again, Mr. Williams," she greets Emery.

Emery nods in acknowledgment. "Nice to see you again," he responds, taking a seat beside Rose and clasping her hand.

He presses a kiss to it as they take off.

"I can't wait for us to arrive. My mum will be so thrilled to meet you!" Emery says with a soft smile.

Rose can't exactly match his enthusiasm. "I think I will sleep the entire flight to ease my nerves," she whispers.

"Okay, the bed is back there," Emery replies, nodding towards the back of the plane.

As soon as their pilot gives the green light, Rose heads straight for the bed. It is midnight at the time of their departure, and after such an eventful day she wants nothing more than to sleep. She leaves Emery with a kiss goodnight.

Emery stays up a little bit more, journaling his thoughts. Sophie makes conversation with him as he writes.

"How have you been?" she begins awkwardly.

Emery smiles politely and looks up at her. "Good. How about you?"

Sophie blushes. "Good. I was hoping I'd see you again. I wasn't sure what happened."

"Happened?" Emery says, confused. "What do you mean?"

"I wasn't sure if you had flown back, maybe on a different aircraft or something," Sophie says softly.

"Oh. No, I just… a lot has happened since I arrived." Emery puts his pen down to give her his full attention.

"She's lovely," Sophie says, referring to Rose as she points to the back of the plane.

"Yes, she is." Emery nods, and his face lights up like that of a man madly in love.

Sophie smiles, but the gesture seems forced. Pained, almost. "She's lucky to have you."

Emery shrugs. "Honestly, I'm the lucky one. She is everything I've ever wished for and more." He looks down at his journal pensively. "She is the love of my life."

Sophie watches him, but her expression grows tighter.

"I wasn't expecting that when I came here, I would find the love of my life. But I have, and it is the best feeling in the world."

She visibly swallows, averting her gaze. "Maybe one day it will happen for me."

Emery can't help but notice a sadness there, and he attempts to reassure her. "I'm sure it will."

He proceeds to get up from his seat to join Rose in bed.

"I will see you in the morning," he says, nodding farewell to the flight attendant.

Sophie murmurs quietly, "Goodnight."

Emery opens the door into the bedroom space, letting

himself in. Rose is already fast asleep. Eager to join her, he swiftly undresses and makes himself comfortable beside her. He touches her softly to let her know he is there with her.

Rose opens her eyes very drowsily and nods but goes back to sleep.

He lets her rest and begins to doze off himself. Emery can't wait to see his mother, to catch up and tell her all about his time in Carmel and everything he has discovered so far. He is most excited for his mother to meet the woman he was seeing in his regression.

His mind races a mile a minute; he worries about people finding out he is back in the country, even more so if they see he is accompanied by a woman. The commotion that would ensue would be a total nightmare for him and Rose. It is her first time visiting, and he hopes they can quickly make it to his family's home without any fuss. There are no guarantees, and all he can do is hope.

Upon arriving in London, Emery begins to fidget with his hair and clothes. Eventually swaying slightly as he stands. Rose can sense the change in his demeanor.

"What's wrong?" Rose asks Emery, frowning in concern.

"Uh. Well, I just hope we're not spotted," Emery says nervously.

"Spotted?" she gapes at him. "How well-known are you here?"

Emery tightens his lips into a thin line. "My family is very well-known. Old money, socialites, that sort of thing. I don't really like to talk about it much, but I must prepare you for what may come. I don't want you to think that I'm hiding anything from you."

Rose stares at Emery, forehead creased. "Okay, now you're scaring me."

"Sorry." He grimaces. "Not my intention."

She shrugs in return. "I sort of feel like I have no idea what I'm walking into. It isn't the best feeling," she admits.

Emery rests his hands on Rose's shoulders. "It'll be alright. I just figured I should give you a heads up."

Rose gazes at him, unsure what to think. Emery takes a deep breath and heads for the front of the aircraft where Sophie stands with the plane door open for them.

"Hello," Emery greets, nervously trying to peer out to see if the coast is clear of any photographers that may be lurking for any socialite, arrivals. Rose follows behind him.

The car is waiting at the bottom of the steps. Emery takes Rose's hand and guides her to the vehicle quickly.

Rose is startled by Emery's hasty lead.

"Bye! Thank you!" Rose says to Sophie as Emery leads her away.

Their driver greets them after putting their luggage in the car. Emery gives him the address to his parents' home. He's nervous but also elated that no one has spotted them. Without hesitation, they drive out of the airport parking lot and off to The William's Estate. Throughout the ride, Rose can sense that Emery is antsy.

"I feel like you're more nervous than I am," Rose says to him with a half-smile.

Emery beams at her. "No, I just... we made it out of the airport. I was worried."

"Oh," Rose remarks, frowning slightly. "Well, it's not like the media knew you were coming."

"No, but they lie in wait." Emery says.

Rose notices on the drive that the neighboring homes are very beautiful and grand, each with their own design. The fine stone on the exterior of some buildings compliments the lush green ivy that climbs up the walls. Large trees surround the estates, allowing only a small peek into the properties.

The massive iron gates all have a small security booth to vet guests before they can reach the long driveways leading up to the front entrance of the homes.

"We are here," Emery finally says, and the driver rolls in past the gates to a prestigious home.

Rose is at a loss for words. She has seen beautiful homes before but nothing like this. This house is in a league of its own. Refined, reflecting classic designs of true English elegance. A monarch would be more than pleased to live here.

"Welcome," Emery says warmly. "I hope they don't have anyone over right now."

Rose begins to feel overwhelmed and unsure of how she will be received by Emery's family and friends. As they approach the main building, she can see cars lining the driveway.

"Oh. Great," Emery mutters sarcastically, a grimace marring his features.

Rose turns to look at him. "What?"

⚜

Emery nods his head in the direction of the Montgomery family's car. "My parents' friends are here."

He knows what a drag it will be to have to introduce Rose to the Montgomerys, given their insistence on him marrying their daughter. Emery would like to give Rose at least a day or two before letting her in on the drama with them.

Elizabeth Montgomery is by no means one to hold back, but if she tries to attack Rose or disrespect her in any way, things will get ugly very quickly.

Chapter 6

E mery takes Rose up to the front door and leads the way
in. Rose gasps quietly as she looks around.

"Oh my God," Rose whispers in awe, taking in the
grandeur of the space. The black and white checkered marble
floors reflect the warm twinkle of the lighting in the room. Fine
China vases filled with the most pristine white roses adorn the
accent tables. Adding a delightful scent of rose to the space.
"What in the world?"

Emery looks around to see if he can find anyone. Nannie
sees Emery first from atop the stairs and can't believe her eyes.
She sets down the towels in her hand on the nearest table and
rushes down to greet him.

"Master Em!" Nannie shouts excitedly. "Master Em! How
lovely to see you!" She jumps up to hug him, laughing happily.

"Nannie!" Emery says back with a smile.

"I didn't know you were coming!" she exclaims.

"I wanted to surprise you all." He shrugs.

"Well, surprised I am!" Nannie remarks. Her large dark
eyes suddenly turn to look at Rose. "Oh, and who might this
be?" she asks, intrigued. "It's been ages since Emery has brought
anyone home. As it is, he's hardly ever home to begin with."

"Nannie, I'd like you to meet Rose," Emery says promptly,
brushing aside her comment.

Rose offers Nannie a beaming smile. "Nice to meet you," she says politely.

Nannie gives Rose a great big hug. "So lovely to meet you, darling! You are beautiful," she exclaims.

Emery can hear his mother and the Montgomerys in the living room area chatting away.

"Oh, God," he mutters under his breath.

Nannie raises her brow at Emery.

"Oh, God, indeed. Ms. Juliet is here with them," she says, whispering.

Emery shakes his head. "Should we wait until they leave? We could go up to the room and get settled before—"

Before Emery can finish his sentence, his mother steps out into the foyer and spots him. She immediately gasps. "Oh my god!" she says excitedly. "Emery!" Victoria runs up to her son and greets him with the warmest of hugs. "Oh, how I've missed you!"

Emery embraces his mother back and nods in Rose's direction. She shifts from one foot to another while rubbing the back of her ear in a self-soothing fashion. But she smiles as she sees that Emery looks just like his mother.

"Mum, this is Rose," Emery explains. "My girlfriend. Rose, this is my mother, Victoria Williams." He nods towards his mother.

Victoria smiles happily at Rose and admires her with wonder. She recalls seeing Rose in the prophetic visions she'd received. "Oh, yes," Victoria says. "Hello, dear."

Rose smiles graciously at her.

Victoria gifts Rose a hug.

"I am so happy to finally meet you. We have very interesting topics to discuss while you two are here," she tells both Emery and Rose with a raised brow.

"Has the other side been talking?" Emery asks his mother, intrigued.

Victoria smirks. "Oh, they have! Always, darling. But "I'll tell you later. I have company now. Won't you two join us in the living room? Or would you rather get settled in first?"

Nannie takes some of the luggage upstairs to Emery's bedroom, pursing her lips as she goes.

A displeased expression washes over Emery's face.

"I would say I'd rather not, but they've likely already heard us," Emery whispers to his mother. To which she agrees and takes the lead, signaling them to follow. "Come on. Let's get this over with." She whispers back.

Emery looks at Rose apologetically and takes her hand. Rose is unsure what to make of it.

Victoria leads the way into the living room where the Montgomerys are waiting perched on the lounge chairs. Emery sees Juliet first and braces himself for what he imagines may be the most awkward moment yet.

Juliet's eyes light up when she sees Emery enter the room, but just as quickly, they dim as she sees Rose trailing behind him, holding his hand. She feels her heart sink into her stomach, the love of her life walking in with another woman.

"Emery!" Mrs. Montgomery says, clearly pleased to see him. "You have been gone so long!"

She rises from her seat to greet him. But she also eyes Rose standing behind Emery and her expression tightens. "Who might this be?" she asks Emery.

She stares at Rose coldly from head to toe. Emery is still holding Rose's hand as he introduces her.

"My girlfriend," Emery states coolly.

The living room grows uncomfortably quiet. Rose smiles at Mrs. Montgomery politely but doesn't receive a smile in return, only serving to further the tension.

Rose stands there lost, unsure of what the silence is all about. Juliet stares at Rose, her heart aching in her chest. She toys with her cup of tea, fighting the urge to run out of the room. This is something out of her worst nightmare.

Clearing his throat, Emery leads Rose to sit beside him on the large sofa.

Mrs. Montgomery watches them with tight lips. Emery grips Rose's hand for support; he understands how uncomfortable this may be.

Emery quickly says hello to Juliet and introduces Rose swiftly.

"Juliet, this is Rose. My girlfriend." He reluctantly says wincing. Emery watches her reaction carefully for any potential early signs of disrespect.

"Nice to meet you." Juliet answers faintly. Her downcast eyes give away the emotional pain she is in.

"Nice to meet you." Rose responds. Clueless to what the tension is about but it doesn't take long for her to figure it out.

Emery can see the hurt in her eyes as she shakes Rose's hand. The timing of their arrival is regrettable, to say the least.

Victoria does her best to lighten the mood by inviting Rose to see her garden. She feels terrible that Rose has been greeted in her home by her guests in such an uncomfortable manner. Emery stays close to Rose, refusing to leave her side.

He can feel Juliet's gaze boring into him. To him, it feels unbearable.

Mr. Montgomery fades into the background, obviously quite uncomfortable himself.

"I apologize for this awkwardness," Victoria whispers to Rose as they walk around the garden, admiring the flora.

Rose nods, unwilling to say much as the Montgomerys trail closely behind them. Juliet watches Emery with Rose, envious of how attentive and protective he is being. She is no fool; Juliet knows Emery is madly in love with Rose. The way he looks at her is the way every woman wants to be looked at.

Juliet and her parents end up staying for dinner. Suffice to say, Mrs. Montgomery wants to find out as much as she can about Rose. She, too, sees how infatuated Emery appears to be with the woman.

She can't hide her disdain as she watches Emery struggle to keep his hands off Rose. In fact, everyone notices the energy between them both. It is intense.

He trails behind Rose like a protective shadow ready to pounce and attack anyone who may attempt to disrespect her. Emery always keeps his hands on her body, and every now and then when he senses her body tense up, he gifts her a gentle squeeze of support. Both as if psychically connected respond to the other's subtle changes in demeanor.

Victoria knew that this moment was coming and had a strong feeling that Emery and Rose would face some envy and jealousy from others by being together.

The dinner table is being prepped while they are all in the garden, taking in the lovely sunshine that is hard to come by in England. Emery plucks one of the red roses from a bush and gifts it to Rose. Delighted by his gesture, she kisses him.

"Thank you," Rose whispers.

The ardent displays of affection between them are becoming too much for Juliet to bear, causing her to stalk off into the house. Mrs. Montgomery wants to follow her daughter but feels it is best to stay in the garden to keep watch over the new couple.

"I think dinner is ready by now," Victoria says to everyone after a few moments of quiet. "Shall we?" She signals everyone back toward the home.

Emery grabs Rose's hand. "Are you alright?" he asks as he kisses her temple.

Rose nods and wraps her arm around his waist.

Rose observes the dining room in awe as they enter.

"This is incredible!" she tells Emery, observing the massive array of delectable foods.

"Yes, my mother has truly outdone herself." He smiles.

Everyone takes their seats. Juliet is seated directly across from Emery, and the tension is felt by all in the room. Victoria shifts in her seat and plays with the flower arrangement in front of her plate to ease her discomfort. Emery tries to avoid eye contact with Juliet. Nevertheless, she continues to stare at him, looking as if she is about to burst into tears any minute.

"Where is Dad?" Emery asks Victoria, trying to lighten the mood and act as if Juliet and her mother are not throwing daggers at him and Rose with their eyes from across the table.

"He's off on a business trip. He'll be back tomorrow," his mother says.

After they've eaten well into their meal, Rose begins to feel tired. She rests her hand on Emery's thigh.

Juliet gazes at Rose, seething with envy. Unaware of Juliet and Emery's history, Rose isn't quite sure what to make of the situation. Rose has come across jealous and envious women before, but this instance takes the cake. She is eager to ask Emery about Juliet.

"So, how did you two meet?" Juliet dares to ask, breaking the tense quiet.

Emery clears his throat uncomfortably. Mrs. Montgomery is ready to listen intently, leaning forward in her seat.

"It's quite complex. I don't wish to discuss that with you," Emery answers her.

Victoria looks down at her plate almost cringing. The tension is unbearable.

"Where did you go? You've been gone a while," Mr. Montgomery asks, trying to shift the conversation away from Juliet as he drinks a sip of wine.

"I went on a getaway to Carmel," Emery replies with a polite smile. He has always liked Mr. Montgomery for the mere fact that he knows not to pry too much into the affairs of other people.

"Oh, I see. I don't believe I've heard of it," he says calmly. "So it was for vacation, not work?"

"I wasn't working," Emery confirms.

Juliet excuses herself.

"Where are you going?" Mrs. Montgomery asks her daughter, brows pinched in concern.

"I've lost my appetite," she mutters under her breath. "I'll be in the piano room if anyone cares."

Emery's body relaxes into his seat as Juliet leaves the table.

"Emery, could you grab me a bottle of wine from the wine cellar please? I didn't bring one out. I didn't know you were coming," his mother says to him.

"Uh, sure. Is it unlocked? Or do I need the key?" he says, rising from his seat.

"It should be unlocked."

Victoria watches as Emery leaves the table, leaving Rose behind with them.

"So, what do you do? For a living?" Mr. Montgomery asks Rose as he takes yet another bite of food.

"I write," Rose answers him simply, tearing apart a bread roll.

"Oh, that's wonderful," he chimes with a grin.

But Mrs. Montgomery stares at Rose, unimpressed. She smirks while she eats her food.

Chapter 7

Emery walks past the piano room where Juliet sits alone. She wipes away a tear as she spots him walk past in a hurry. Seeing he is headed for the cellar, she follows him.

"Emery," she calls to him, trailing after him into the cellar. Emery looks back in surprise.

"Is it serious?" she presses. "Are you in love with her?"

Emery sighs. "Why do you ask? Juliet, we have been through this."

Her eyes water as she watches him. "I refuse to lose all hope."

"God, I really don't want to hurt you. Juliet, I wish you'd give up."

"It's not as if I can stop loving you, Emery. After all these years, I thought we were destined to be together. Everyone else thought so, too." She sniffles.

Tired of the same old conversations with Juliet, Emery looks down at his feet. Letting out a frustrated sigh, he says to her, "Just because we are childhood friends that grew up together doesn't mean we would end up together or that we should."

Emery walks up to Juliet, completely over the conversation.

"I am madly in love with Rose. She is the woman I will

marry," he asserts. "So, to answer your question, yes, it is. *Very* serious. There was never a future for us, Juliet."

Juliet nods her head, swallowing hard. "Why didn't you want to tell me how you met?" she asks. "It isn't an intrusive question; everyone asks that."

Emery glares at Juliet, now annoyed. "Because I don't want to. It's that simple."

He walks back to the dining room after fetching the bottle, leaving Juliet standing in the cellar alone.

Rose turns to look at Emery, relieved that he is back. Victoria had been steering Mrs. Montgomery's probing questions away from her in his absence. "There you are!" Victoria says to her son, her arms out seeking the wine.

Emery hands it to her. "Sorry, got held up," he says, giving her a wide-eyed look.

Mrs. Montgomery notices and assumes Juliet spoke to him.

After dinner, the Montgomerys head home. The night ends very tense. Victoria walks them out to their car. Though she's trying to be as diplomatic as possible, she is glad to see them leave. The evening has been too awkward, even for her.

Victoria is incredibly talented at keeping the peace. As the Montgomerys drive away, Elizabeth Montgomery turns to look at her daughter as they both sit in the back seat.

"Don't you worry, this isn't over," she says haughtily, raising her chin.

Juliet shakes her head in despair. Her eyes fill with tears. "It is over, Mother. I spoke to Emery." She wipes away a tear.

Elizabeth Montgomery turns her daughter's face to look at her, narrowing her eyes.

"He is determined to marry her." Juliet relays. Her voice breaks as she utters the words.

"No, he won't. You wait and see, I'll find something. Once

he sees how out of place she is in our world, they'll break apart."
Elizabeth tsks.

"Elizabeth!" Jack Montgomery shouts as he drives, glaring
at her through the rearview mirror. "I will not have you stirring
up trouble! I forbid it."

She ignores him completely, rolling her eyes. Elizabeth
Montgomery is hell-bent on causing trouble. She hatches a plan
to dig into Rose's past and find out what she can about her.
Elizabeth phones her social circle to turn them all against Rose
before they have even had a chance to meet her.

"We will push her out," she whispers to Juliet. "You'll see.
This is far from over."

✿❀❀

Back at The Williams Estate, Victoria finally gets Emery and
Rose to herself.

"We have much to discuss!" she says happily, returning to
the living room after escorting the Montgomerys out.

"That was so painful!" Emery blurts with a groan.

Rose nods in agreement. "Yeah, what was up with them?"
she asks now that they can speak freely.

"Juliet has been madly in love with Emery ever since they
were kids. They are family friends," Victoria explains, taking a
seat in the single wingback chair beside Rose. She's delighted to
have her in front of her. Victoria admires the way Emery and
Rose look together. *They are a natural pair* she thinks to herself.

A surprised look comes over Rose's face. "Well, that makes
a lot of sense now." She turns to look at Emery. "And you didn't
tell me," she says accusingly.

Emery shakes his head, preparing to defend himself. "Baby,
I didn't know they were going to be here."

Rose rolls her eyes. "Her mom didn't seem very nice either.
She kept asking me so many questions at dinner."

"She's a very peculiar woman," Emery sighs.

"Elizabeth Montgomery was hoping Emery would marry her daughter," Victoria adds. "So, that's why she was just as upset as Juliet. I bet they were quite in shock to see you here with Emery."

He slumps back into the sofa, drained from the evening. "She confronted me in the wine cellar, as well."

Victoria raises a brow. "Did she?"

Emery nods. "Yes."

"What did she tell you?" Rose asks, leaning closer.

"She asked me if I was serious about you. I told her yes, and she told me that she would never lose hope about being with me."

Much to her surprise, Rose glares at Emery her body leans towards him while she lays a possessive hand on his thigh. "Lovely," she retorts sarcastically.

"Emery, I noticed you became very upset when Juliet asked how you two met," Victoria remarks.

Emery raises a brow at his mother. "Why, do you think? If I had said how we met, that's too much to get into. Also, the fact that Rose is still married, that would've been a fiasco."

Victoria almost spits out her tea.

"Yes, there is that," she says promptly, dabbing her lips with a handkerchief. "Don't want them making a big deal out of that. I know they would, as they love to gossip." Victoria gives Rose a tight smile. "I want to apologize for them," she says. "Truly."

"It's okay. This wasn't planned to happen. Besides, what does she expect? Just because she wants to marry Emery doesn't mean he should. He has a say in his own love life. She will be okay." Rose shrugs.

"I'm just concerned they're plotting something," Emery says. "They won't let up that easy."

"Well, that makes me feel so much better," Rose retorts, grimacing.

Victoria sips her tea quietly. She hopes Emery and Rose are pulled closer together rather than apart. Should people try anything, it isn't just the Montgomerys Rose and Emery should be worried about. It is everyone else, too.

She knows all too well the way things operate in their world. If someone is not liked or well accepted, they will try and push them out. Elizabeth is a snob; Victoria knows she doesn't approve of Rose already because of her background.

Nonetheless, she will do what she can to protect Rose from the vultures.

After a while, they finally call it a night. Both Emery and Rose are exhausted, so Emery leads Rose to his bedroom.

"God, I wish that hadn't happened," he blurts out as soon as he closes the door behind them. "I'm telling you, it was so painful!" he laments.

"You're telling me? You left me alone with them at the dinner table!"

"I was getting the wine my mum wanted. It's not like I wanted to leave. What was I supposed to do, ask you to come with me? It would've looked odd."

Rose rolls her eyes and undresses for bed. She slips under the covers naked; he quickly follows her lead.

"What else happened in the wine cellar?" Rose presses.

Emery grips Rose's body and pulls her towards him. "Nothing else that matters," he whispers. Nestling his mouth between her thighs, his tongue spoils her with delight as it finds its home within her.

Her hands grip onto his, locking her in place on the bed. Rose grinds her hips towards him. Her legs fall wide open to accommodate Emery.

Her delicate hands move to grip his tussled dark hair as she breathlessly moans, surrendering deeper into his clutches. With every moan elicited from Rose, his penis becomes harder and more erect. He wants to devour her body and soul.

Emery takes command and rises from between her sweet legs to position himself. He pulls her closer to his awaiting and eager penis. Emery delights in the way her long, dark, and disheveled hair looks on his bed, her pale complexion now flushed.

Her hazel eyes drunkenly gaze at him as he takes her leg and rests her ankle on his shoulder. She wraps her other leg around him, pleading for him to fuck her, but he lives to tease her.

"I want you to say it," Emery commands.

"Fuck me," Rose declares, her feverish desire for him unraveling as time ticks by.

Emery takes her as she requests. His thrusts are assertive and powerful, and she welcomes them further by gripping his lower back fervently.

Emery moves to lie directly on top of her, his lips brushing up against her neck. He loves to hear her moan his name longingly in his ear. Rose nears the finish line, her hands digging into his shoulders as she explosively orgasms.

Emery's eyes widen as he lets out a low gasp. As he pulls himself out of her, he makes a mess on the sheets, gripping his shaft as he comes.

Rose kisses him without restraint as he finishes. Emery revels in her pleasure, his hands holding her body against his. A fervent, sweaty mess together, they lie in the sheets, completely undone.

Chapter 8

The following morning, Emery rises before Rose to shower, spellbound and energized from the night before.

He heads downstairs to speak to his mother. He knows she will be watching the sunrise from the garden. She enjoys pruning the roses early before everyone else wakes up.

Emery makes himself a tea and finds his mother amongst the roses as expected.

"Good morning," Victoria tells him, glancing up from her task. "You're up early. I figured you would want to sleep in."

Emery smiles. "Morning."

"Your father will be here at noon."

"Good to know. I look forward to seeing him." He nods.

Victoria adds a few roses to her basket for the vases in her kitchen.

"I wanted to ask you, what do you think about me proposing to Rose here? In this garden of yours," Emery says after a moment.

Victoria is not surprised at all by the news. She knew all this would happen quickly. "I'm happy to hear it. I think it's a lovely idea. Do you know if she will say yes?"

Emery looks down at the tea in his hand. "I hope so. Things are still a bit complicated. Legally, I mean."

"You mean she's still technically married," Victoria supplies.

Emery gives her a tight smile. She pauses, standing up to face him directly.

"How did you two meet?" Victoria raises her brow suspiciously at her son. "Don't lie to me. Did you go about it ethically? You know what your guides told you."

Emery looks away. "I—"

"Emery, must I remind you that if you go about this the wrong way, there will be hell to pay? This is a second chance you are getting to learn. Are you passing or are you failing?" she challenges, narrowing her eyes at him.

"It's not that simple! She is my destined soulmate. We are *destined* to be together. How else am I supposed to go about things? She made the choice. I didn't coerce her into it or anything."

"I'd be curious to see what her husband has to say about that. Does he think you are behaving ethically?" Victoria observes her son suspiciously. She isn't convinced that Emery took the high moral road completely. "You sought Rose out, didn't you?"

Emery smirks. "I couldn't help myself. How else are we supposed to be together?"

"Well, her marriage was already over. You could've stayed out of the picture and given her and the husband a chance to sort it out themselves. Instead, you went and inserted yourself."

"What?!" Emery blurts out, pacing back and forth and runs his hand through his hair. He shakes his head disagreeing with a visible frown.

"Her husband, I assume, is Pierre. If you fail, you will keep all of you stuck in this karmic circle! Emery, I don't think you understand the seriousness of this." Victoria tuts.

"Mum," Emery begins trying to defend himself.

She shakes her head in disapproval. "You are meant to be together, but I told you to let her sort it out. You could've waited for things to naturally fall apart with her husband before coming closer to her. You got impatient."

Emery knows his mother is right but continues to plead his case. "I couldn't stay away from her even if I tried. Once I saw her, it was over," Emery says softly.

Victoria sighs. "Well, I will say a little prayer for you," she retorts.

Emery finishes his tea as he watches his mother continue her work in the garden. The sun is rising, illuminating the well-pruned foliage. In his mind's eye, he envisions exactly how he will propose to Rose, and a powerful emotion fills his heart.

The love he feels for Rose, he has never felt for anyone. She is the love of his life. If she says yes to him. Rose would make him the happiest man in all existence. If only he could find the ring he had given her in their past life together. His friend Theodore is looking for it, he thinks to himself. Maybe he will point him in the right direction.

Victoria watches the sunrise and inhales a deep breath. "Isn't this lovely?" she whispers to herself.

Emery makes his way inside to deliver his now empty teacup to the kitchen sink where he finds Nannie washing dishes.

"Good morning to you," Nannie says quietly, since it is still early.

"Morning," Emery greets, reaching for the dish sponge.

"No," Nannie chides, swatting him away. "I'll do it."

Emery shakes his head. "I've got it."

Nannie places her hands on her hips. "Not while I am here."

"Nannie," Emery says with a sigh. "It's just a cup! I'll do it."

Nannie grips the sponge firmly and holds it away from Emery. "Your grandparents are arriving today, with your father," she says, trying to distract Emery.

"Oh, are they?" His eyes widen at her admission.

Nannie nods.

"That's great. I can't wait to see them. It's been ages!" Emery says with a smile.

He gives Nannie a kiss on the head, then escorts himself back to his room where Rose lies fast asleep. Snuggling in bed with her, he lets out a contented sigh.

Several minutes later, he hears a knock on the door.

"Master Em," Nannie's voice says on the other side.

Emery hops up from bed to open the door slightly. His piercing blue eyes peer at Nannie standing before him holding roses.

"These are for Rose; your mother prepared them for her to place by her bedside," Nannie whispers, glancing at a still-sleeping Rose.

Emery takes the vase from her. "Thank you." She nods as she closes the door.

After he sets the vase of flowers down, Emery can hear someone on the driveway. He walks over to his bedroom window to see who it may be.

Ferdi has pulled up with his father and grandparents in tow. He smiles gleefully, excited to see them. All four make their way into the home, making quite a bit of a fuss. Nannie and Victoria walk over to greet them.

"You're home," Victoria says to Ashby, kissing him lovingly. "I missed you."

Nannie assists Ferdi with their luggage.

"Where is our grandson?" Sir Ashby's mother blurts out. "Please tell me he's here."

"You know he travels a lot," Emery's grandfather says to his wife. "Most likely not."

"Actually" Victoria says, "he *is* here."

Emery's grandmother, Alice, gasps happily. "Oh, I must see him!" she exclaims.

"Yes, I'm sure he will come down soon. He just arrived a day ago."

Sir Ashby raises his brows at Victoria. "Excellent. I need to speak with him about his responsibilities around here," he says sternly.

Victoria shakes her head at him. "I'm afraid now isn't a good time. He's brought someone with him."

Astonished, everyone looks at her, eagerly waiting for her to say who.

"Someone special," Victoria says excitedly. "You'll meet her when they both come down."

"Come on now, breakfast is about to be served," Nannie urges, rushing in.

Chapter 9

As Emery's family all sit in the dining room enjoying breakfast together, they all highly anticipate the moment Emery shows himself. Upstairs, Rose anxiously picks out a dress to wear, Emery can sense her nervousness.

"You have nothing to worry about. They'll love you," Emery assures her.

Rose shakes her head, unconvinced.

"I don't know. From what I'm finding out, you are a highly desired person. I can only imagine some people won't be too fond of me being the one you're choosing."

Emery shrugs. "Not my family, but others, yes. I can't lie."

"Great," Rose sarcastically mutters.

A pensive Emery gazes down at his feet as he recalls the conversation he and his mother had in the rose garden, about Rose still being married. It is something he plans to conceal for as long as he can; rather, he hopes no one will ever have to know.

He knows people love to gossip, Emery is hell-bent on protecting what he and Rose have. Perhaps his mother is right; perhaps he shouldn't have inserted himself in Rose's life the way he did.

But his intentions and feelings for her are pure. He knows

that in his heart, as flawed as his methods may be, he loves her more than anything.

Emery and Rose finally head downstairs, hand in hand. He squeezes hers, attempting to ease some of her nerves. She turns her gaze to him and lets him lead the way. Rose can hear Emery's family loudly chatting in the dining room.

When they walk in, Alice, Emery's grandmother, stops talking and rises from her seat.

"Emery!" she exclaims excitedly, over the moon to see him. "It's been so long!"

She rushes over to hug Emery; Rose stands beside them, waiting for Emery to introduce her.

"And who might this be?" Alice says curiously as she looks wondrously at Rose.

The entire room's gaze is now fixed upon her. Rose uncomfortably glances around, completely despising the fact that all the attention is on her.

"Grandmother, I'd like you to meet Rose," Emery says confidently. "My girlfriend."

Alice's eyes widen. She looks at Emery and back at Rose. "Really?"

Victoria sits at the head of the table, observing. Her large cup of tea almost covers her face while she takes a sip.

Emery nods. "Hello," he says to everyone else in the room, waving from where he stands.

Alice gifts Rose a warm hug. "Well, nice to meet you. I'm sorry I'm short for words, but Emery hasn't brought anyone over in ages!"

Rose smiles politely at Alice. "It's nice to meet you."

"We were beginning to worry," Emery's grandfather blurts out from where he sits. "All he cares about is his work. I'm starting to wonder if we will see anything more from him."

Alice turns to look at her husband, with a scowl.

"Oh, hush!" she tells him, scrunching her nose in distaste.

Rose and Emery take their seats at the table. Emery introduces her formally to his father and grandfather. Sir Ashby is charmed by Rose; he can tell Emery is besotted. He has never seen his son so infatuated with anyone before.

Victoria is eager to experience the moments to come. While Emery and Rose are there, she can speak to both about their past life regressions and what they have discovered so far without her. If they wish, they can continue digging for more information about their shared past.

But Victoria knows her son struggles with darker emotions when it comes to Rose. His jealous, possessive, and controlling tendencies surface. If he cannot overcome these impulses, they have no chance at breaking their karmic loop. The past will most likely be repeated, and Emery will lose Rose forever.

It is imperative Victoria guides Emery if he wishes to be successful.

Emery's family is lovely to Rose; all are incredibly welcoming and loving. But they know very well what is to come if she is to be a permanent fixture in Emery's life. It isn't difficult to see that there will be some challenges down the road.

Alice excuses herself from the table after finishing her breakfast.

"I'm going to go have a rest. Settle in, I'll be back later," she tells the room.

"Would you like me to escort you?" Nannie asks Alice.

"No, no. I'm fine. Thank you," she says softly. "I'll be seeing you later too, young lady," she quips at Rose. "We will have time to get better acquainted." Alice winks mischievously as she walks past.

After breakfast, Sir Ashby takes hold of Emery and gets him

to follow him into his study to have a serious conversation about his future. Rose stays with Victoria and Emery's grandfather in the living room.

"Have a seat," Sir Ashby instructs Emery while he closes the door behind him.

Emery already knows what his father must want to talk about. He is determined to make it abundantly clear that he will do what he wants, not what his father expects of him.

"My time has come; I am retiring, and I need you to take over," Sir Ashby begins.

Emery furrows his brows, a tick in his jaw already forming. "I thought you understood!" he snaps.

"You are not going to get out of this!" Sir Ashby responds, voice stern. "This is your duty. Every Williams takes over, then the next and the next. It's the way it has always been."

Emery shakes his head with a scoff. "You would take away my freedom? My 'duty' is a death sentence. Might as well kill me now!"

Sir Ashby Rolls his eyes. "Oh, don't be so dramatic!" he retorts, waving off his concerns. "This is your responsibility. It is time to grow up."

"Is this what you call growing up? Abandoning myself for the family legacy?" Emery mutters.

"Yes, it is your responsibility to continue it, and after you, your children's."

Emery shakes his head. "No, they will be free to choose for themselves what they want for their life." Of that, he will make certain.

Sir Ashby frowns and places his hands in his pockets. "You enjoy using the family's money. It is only right that you do your share and put your time in."

"If that's the deal, keep your money," Emery snaps back. "I have my own."

"Emery!" Sir Ashby exclaims. "You will do this!"

Emery's piercing gaze glares at his father from where he sits. Sir Ashby and Emery are locked into a battle of wills for the time being.

"I have my future mapped out, and that includes Rose. We will most likely not live here," Emery tells his father sternly.

Sir Ashby can see Emery is madly in love with Rose, but he had no idea he was so serious. Especially not so soon. "You plan to marry this woman?" he demands.

"Of course," Emery says quickly. "I love her."

Sir Ashby stares at his son, taken aback by what he is hearing. "How soon do you plan to marry?" he presses.

Emery looks down at his feet, annoyed by his father's questioning.

"I don't know, I haven't proposed," he reluctantly responds.

"This is a big deal—"

"I know it is," Emery cuts in. "But I have never been more certain of anything my entire life. She is the one."

Chapter 10

After their quarrel, Emery and his father sullenly join the others in the living room. Both act as though they hadn't just argued a few moments ago.

Emery sits down beside Rose and gently rests a hand on her thigh. Sir Ashby watches Emery's demeanor with Rose and glances over at his wife. Victoria gazes at Sir Ashby, unamused.

"Did you have a lovely shouting match?" she asks him slyly.

Sir Ashby averts his gaze. "Could you hear us from out here?"

"Of course," Victoria replies, turning up her chin. "It was muffled, but a few words here and there." She shrugs.

Emery sits there without a care in the world, but soon he finds a way to quickly escape the room,

"I must show you something!" Emery says to Rose, remembering the dusty box he had found at the old, abandoned estate with his friend Theodore. "Come, come," he urges.

Rose follows right behind him as Emery leads her into the library where his mother conducted one of his first past life regressions.

"Close your eyes," Emery commands.

"Is it that serious?" Rose asks with a small smile.

"Just close them," he insists.

Rose obeys, closing her eyes. She can faintly hear Emery shuffling about the room before he comes to stand in front of her.

"Open them."

When she does, she finds a dusty old box in Emery's hands.

"What is this?" Rose asks, confused.

"Look inside." He nods towards the box.

As she peers inside the lid, she can see a miniature portrait.

"Where did you get this?" Rose exclaims in shock. Her hands shake while she holds the old portrait of her former self in her hands. "I can't believe this is real," she whispers to herself.

Emery watches her expression as she struggles to make sense of it all.

"This is…" Rose begins and stops. "I need to sit down."

Emery guides her over to the sofa as they continue looking at the items in the box. Rose continues to stare at the portrait in her hand, swallowing hard. Emery pulls out the old flintlock pistol then, and Rose's eyes expand in horror.

"Oh my god!" Is this—?" she gasps, and Emery nods.

The gun that Emery's former self used to kill Pierre is residing in her hands, proving to be astonishing physical proof. It is one thing to witness certain things of the past, but to hold them in present time in her very hands is surreal.

They sit there for a moment in silence, looking at one another, a moment that would prove to alter their outlook on life forever. Their relationship is a bigger deal than both realize; through their findings, they discover that life is not what they thought it was. Having witnessed what they have in their individual regressions, Rose now sees there is actual physical proof that they did in fact exist in the 18th century as Emmett and Helena.

"I discovered this with my friend Theodore. He is looking

for an emerald ring as well, like the one you had in the past as Helena. I believe it is the very same," Emery explains quietly.

Rose stands up in disbelief.

"An emerald ring?" she asks, making the connection she hadn't before.

"Yes, why?" he glances at her inquiringly.

"Phillip is looking for an emerald ring like the one you are talking about. He hired a man named Theodore to look for it. Well, he did a while ago."

Emery stops talking and stares at Rose, bewildered by what he is hearing.

"Phillip wanted to gift it to me," Rose whispers.

Emery rolls his eyes and shakes his head, he tightens his jaw jealous to learn that Phillip was planning to gift Rose the ring his former self had gifted Helena in the past. The ring is incredibly special and such a symbol of their love. The thought of Theodore finding it for Phillip makes his skin crawl.

"I need to make a call," Emery says with urgency, getting up from where he sits.

Rose numbly stands there in the library, processing the items in front of her. The miniature portrait of Helena, her former-self, and the flintlock pistol.

After departing the room, Emery calls his friend Theodore and asks him if he has found the emerald. Much to Emery's relief, he hasn't had any luck. But Emery knows the clock is ticking; Theodore most likely isn't the only person looking for it.

The search for the ring begins to become an obsession for Emery. He won't rest until he finds it; in his mind, Emery has pictured himself proposing to Rose with it.

Victoria walks in to see Rose with the flintlock pistol in her hand, speechless.

She sits beside Rose slowly, careful not to startle her as she awaits an explanation.

"Emery found this box and the items inside such as the gun, the portrait, and a few other pieces of paper in there before you met. I took it upon myself to conduct a past life regression for him," Victoria says softly. "That's when he saw you."

Rose turns to look at Victoria, hanging on her every word.

"One discovery led to another, and he followed his intuition… to you. But I need to ask you," Victoria whispers. She peers around to make sure Emery won't hear while he stands in the hallway on his phone. "How did you two meet? Did Emery insert himself in your life?"

"I…" Rose begins.

"The truth, Rose. It is very important. You mustn't repeat the past." Victoria warns.

"Well, It's a long story. But you could say it was a process."

Victoria listens to Rose closely. "I was undergoing past life regressions on my own and kept seeing Emery," Rose says. "He eventually started seeing Catherine, too, and bought a house a few houses down from mine."

Victoria looks over at the hall, pursing her lips. "He bought a house so close to you?"

"Yes." Rose nods. "I don't think he knew I lived down the street from him, of course. We met on the beach at night, initially, and then he showed up to my astrology class."

Victoria throws daggers Emery's way, tutting in disappointment. "Hmm…"

"What?" Rose asks curiously.

Victoria sighs. "It's just that with the history between you, it is imperative that the past is not repeated. Emery must allow you to make the choice on your own. He mustn't coerce you into choosing him."

Rose looks at Victoria with rapt attention.

"He robbed you of a choice in the past life that is resurfacing now, when Emmett killed Pierre. Love is freedom, not bondage. No matter how much you love someone, you must let them be free to make their own choice."

Victoria looks down at the pistol in Rose's hands.

"He failed to do that in the past, and it has locked you into this karmic wheel," she finishes.

"What if I've made my choice?" Rose asks, her gaze roving around the library as she contemplates this.

Victoria taps into Rose's energy. "Have you?" she presses, unconvinced.

Rose stares at Victoria, unsure of what she means.

Victoria cracks a small smile. "Emery told you, right?"

Rose glances back toward the hallway, then back at Victoria. "Told me what?"

"Let's just say, I can see with more than just my eyes."

"Oh! Your gifts," Rose exclaims with a chuckle. "Yes, he has."

"And I sense that you still hold some reservations about him. The same way you did in the past. There is work to be done on your end, too. You must choose. Do so wholeheartedly and stick with your decision. Indecisiveness isn't good. You are learning to trust your heart over your mind," Victoria explains with reverence. "*That* is your lesson. Your indecisiveness causes pain for others. Everyone shares some blame in the situation from the past life."

Chapter 11

"I can help you both find more items," Victoria says, standing up from where she sits in the library. "There is so much more to discover about that past life."

Victoria takes the miniature portrait in her hands and gazes at it with a glimmer in her eyes.

"Isn't that a marvel? You look the same," she remarks.

Rose nods. "Emery is looking for the emerald ring," she says quietly.

"I see. Many people are. The emerald is incredibly rare and worth a lot of money."

"Do you have a hunch as to where it could be?" Rose asks, hoping Victoria can get some guidance from *the other side.*

"From what I know, the last known place the ring was seen was on the island Emmett and Helena fled to after Pierre's death. After that, the trail from the other side grows cold," Victoria answers with a shrug.

"How much more is there to the past?" Rose asks. "Can you help us with the regressions?"

Victoria smiles at her, letting out a little squeal. "A bit more."

Emery walks back into the room moments later, restless.

"Theodore hasn't found the ring, has he?" Victoria says to him with a knowing look.

"Ring?" Emery asks, bewildered that she'd mention it. "Oh, no he has not, thankfully. Did Rose tell you about it?"

Victoria turns her gaze towards Rose. "About how you were not completely honest with me about how you two met?" she drawls, shifting her eyes to glare at Emery.

"Mum," Emery groans, about to start defending himself. She quickly shakes her head to dismiss him.

"Anyway," he sighs. "Phillip, Rose's soon-to-be-ex-husband, is the doctor in the United States who contracted Theodore to find the emerald ring for him."

"Come again?" Victoria says, stunned.

"Yup." Emery nods.

"Wow, fate wasn't messing around when it weaved you all together," Victoria chuckles darkly.

"Unfortunately," Emery laments, moving to lean against a nearby bookshelf.

"Would you like to continue the regressions here?" Victoria asks him. "I'm more than happy to assist you two while you're here."

Emery nods. "That would probably help."

"Excellent. Maybe this will help us find the ring." She claps.

Sir Ashby walks in with Emery's grandfather. Without prompting, Victoria takes the box from Rose and puts it away.

Emery's father looks at him, still upset at his unwillingness to fulfill his obligations and prefers to not speak with him at all. Much like children, they both ignore one another when either one adds anything to the conversation with the others.

Rose and Victoria smirk as they observe Sir Ashby and Emery continuing with their nonsense.

Victoria excuses herself but grabs Rose's hand and takes her along, leaving Emery behind with his father and grandfather.

Emery moves to quickly follow behind his mother and Rose.

"Emery, do you mind? I wish to speak with Rose privately," Victoria says to him over her shoulder.

Taken aback, Emery stammers. "Are… Are you sure?"

Victoria nods, with Rose on her arm as they pause by the door.

Reluctantly, Emery sits over in one of the lounge chairs.

Sir Ashby glances at Emery, confused. "Whatever it is must be important," he says to Emery.

Emery says nothing and looks down at his feet, disappointed he's not included.

"Well, my boy!" Emery's grandfather begins gleefully. "What are your plans while here?" He laughs as he sits beside his grandson.

Emery grins. "Doing a bit of research. I think," he answers.

His grandfather furrows his eyebrows. "Research?" Emery nods. "What kind? For work?"

"Something like that," Emery says, glancing around the old library.

"Are you ever not working? Give it a rest, my boy!" his grandfather says with a laugh.

Emery looks over at his father uncomfortably.

Sir Ashby assumes quietly it must have to do with Rose and the past life regressions Victoria had been assisting Emery with before he left.

With perfect timing, Nannie walks in pushing a golden trolly with brandy and cigars, helping to alleviate the stuffiness in the room.

"Excellent, Nannie!" Emery's grandfather says with glee.

Nannie hands Sir Ashby a cigar and lighter. He pulls out his cigar cutter from the left breast pocket of his suit to which Emery makes a face.

"How can you smoke those things? They're disgusting and bad for your health!"

Sir Ashby looks at his son with a gleam in his eye.

"We all have our vices," he says after he gives his cigar a puff, smirking. "Yours just happens to be a person."

Emery's face grows stern. His piercing blue eyes glare at his father. Nannie helps Emery's grandfather with his cigar and brandy. Her large dark eyes glance over at Emery. After assisting his grandfather, she hands Emery a glass.

"Thank you, Nannie." He takes the glass from her. "I'll pour it myself, thank you," he says to her softly.

"No, No. Don't be ridiculous. I'm happy to do it," Nannie chides with a smile, taking care of his drink. "I'm very happy you are home."

"Yes! We all are," Emery's grandfather chimes in. "And how long will you be staying?"

"I'm not sure, possibly a month," Emery muses.

"Wonderful!" Nannie says, beaming. "Well, gentlemen if you don't need anything else from me, I'll be off."

All nod and thank Nannie.

"So, tell me about Rose," Emery's grandfather asks him once she's gone. "Is it serious?"

He raises his brows, eager for an answer. His only grandchild finally marrying? What a delight, if so!

Emery clears his throat awkwardly. He looks away from his father and down at his feet for a second. "Very," Emery begins. "She's the love of my life."

Emery's grandfather lets out a cheerful laugh. "How amazing! Have you thought of proposing while you're here?"

Sir Ashby watches Emery without saying much. He withholds the fact that Victoria told him everything, the situation with Rose still being married, and Emery moving things along quickly, not caring for any consequences his thoughtless actions could have.

It would be quite the scandal if the public knew that Emery Williams, the most eligible bachelor and only heir to the Williams fortune, is having an affair with a still very married woman. Sir Ashby couldn't have guessed how far his son was willing to go to have Rose. He knows his son, of course; he is of high moral character and is incredibly honest, cool, and collected. But this man sitting in front of him? He does not recognize.

He observes the change in Emery, seeing he is beyond infatuated with Rose, and from what Victoria has told him about their past, Sir Ashby also fears Emery may not be able to control his darker tendencies.

He fears he may fail to break out of the karmic cycle he landed himself in all those many years ago in his past life.

"She's very beautiful," his grandfather says to both gentlemen, taking a sip of brandy.

Emery smirks, nodding toward him in thanks.

"Very beautiful," Sir Ashby says in agreement. "Do you really plan to propose to her while you're here?"

Emery turns to his father. "Yes."

"Have you chosen a ring yet?" his grandfather asks.

"I have something in mind, but nothing is set in stone yet." He shrugs.

"Well, my boy; we have plenty of family heirlooms. I'm sure one of those rings will do just fine unless you want to create something special. That's lovely, too." His grandfather beams.

"Yes, I'll have a look," Emery says with a nod. "But I've seen the collection before, and nothing stands out to me that I can remember."

Emery's grandfather takes a puff from his cigar and sets it down as he exhales, filling the area with a cloud of smoke. "I'll have a look. I don't think you have seen them all."

Chapter 12

Emery leaves his grandfather and father to go investigate where his mother and Rose have wandered off to. He struggles to find them; they're not in the garden, nor in the kitchen, nor the living room.

He takes the stairs and can hear his mother's voice coming from her room on the second floor. He can hardly make out what she is saying. Her voice is faint and muffled by the closed bedroom door. As he puts his ear up to the door, he hears more clearly.

"Three, two, one. Come back all the way, and when you are ready, open your eyes."

Emery is surprised that his mother is guiding a regression on Rose. *Why?* he wonders.

He softly knocks, awaiting entry.

"Come in," Victoria beckons, walking towards the door to open it. But Emery opens it before she can reach the knob. Emery glimpses Rose slowly opening her eyes and can see she has been crying.

"Is everything alright?" Emery asks, growing concerned.

"Yes, of course," Victoria assures him.

"You've been gone for hours," Emery reminds her, releasing a sigh, he bites his lip impatiently. His eyes fixed on Rose longingly.

"Oh, you'll be alright. A few hours apart won't kill you," Victoria quips back.

Emery quickly makes his way to Rose as she slowly gets up from Victoria's bed.

"Are you alright? You've been crying," he murmurs.

Rose tentatively looks into Emery's eyes.

"What's wrong?"

Rose glances at Victoria as tears fill, they begin to spill down her cheeks.

"What?" Emery demands, turning to look at his mother. "Can someone please tell me what is going on?"

Victoria shakes her head. "I think that is for Rose to decide."

Emery turns to Rose. "Will you tell me?" he presses.

Rose shakes her head, sniffling. "I don't want to speak of it just now. Please understand, I must process."

Emery nods and holds her as she cries in his arms. Victoria leaves them to offer some privacy.

The session that just concluded was led by Rose's guides. They instructed Victoria to assist. It was no regression at all, but a *progression*. A peek into the future, one Rose wishes now she could unsee.

Rose's emotional reaction after her session with his mother sends a shiver down Emery's spine. *What could Rose have seen that made her so upset?* he thinks to himself.

"Let's go to our room," Emery suggests, still holding Rose.

She nods and walks with Emery to his bedroom.

As the days pass, Rose tries to calm herself, but she grows more restless. Emery senses a change in her, and it makes him anxious. But he doesn't want to press Rose for answers. Yet as time goes on, Rose withdraws further and further into herself.

Emery begins to feel the emotional distance between them, and it becomes unbearable.

Confused, all he can think to blame is his mother. He angrily confronts her a week after her session with Rose one evening after dinner.

"What did she see?" Emery demands, his hands clenched into fists at his sides. He quickly follows his mother into the garden, unable to go on any longer without answers.

Victoria looks anywhere except at Emery, refusing to meet his gaze.

"Tell me!" he shouts in desperation. "What did she see?"

Victoria finally turns her apprehensive gaze towards Emery.

"Please," Emery pleads. "I simply cannot lose her. What did she see, Mum?"

"I can't help you Emery. I mustn't tell." Her lips thin into a sad smile.

Emery rests his trembling hand on his heaving chest. He paces back and forth as if uncomfortable in his own body; he can't stand it. His hands shake nervously as he struggles to guess what could have gone wrong. The ugly sinking sensation in his stomach is brutal.

Agony is written all over his face as his heart beats away furiously in his chest. His joyful future he had imagined with the love of his life is in jeopardy.

Emery struggles to stop himself from crying, but the fear he feels is too great.

Sir Ashby comes out to see what the fuss is about.

"Emery," Sir Ashby says carefully as he approaches. Wrinkling his forehead He, too, looks concerned by his son's demeanor.

Victoria sees Emmett, Emery's old self from his old 18th century lifetime in front of her, instead of Emery. He has soul work to do, or he will be doomed to repeat the past, causing pain and despair not only for himself but everyone involved.

His relationship with Rose depends on it. If they are to stay together, Emery must change his relationship behavior and heal.

Sir Ashby places his hands on his son's shoulders firmly. "Calm down," he says to him. "If your mother can't tell you what she saw, you must respect that."

Emery jerks his shoulders free of his father's grip and stomps off to the library without another word.

Victoria shakes her head with a sigh, pinching the bridge of her nose.

"Are you okay?" Sir Ashby asks.

Victoria nods, dropping her hand to look at him. "I'm just worried, is all."

The following day, Victoria and Rose sneak off to the library and conduct a regression to see the past once more. The session before allowed them to see the future, a potential outcome. Now, they must learn from past mistakes.

Sir Ashby aided Victoria in taking Emery out of the house so that he would not interrupt. She knows he will want to know more about Rose's regressions and would be an incessant pain in the ass.

As the two women shuffle into the library, Victoria quickly sits in her chair, just as eager as Rose to find out more information about the past.

Notepad and pen in hand, Victoria says to Rose, "I'm ready when you are."

Rose lays down on the couch and takes several deep breaths after closing her eyes.

Victoria begins counting down per usual. Her soft voice allows for Rose to relax and go deep into hypnosis. Within seconds, her consciousness is transported to a life far from this one.

The guides bring her to the aftermath of Pierre's death. Rose is immersed in the moment, which allows her to completely feel all her old emotions.

Victoria watches as Rose's breathing changes from calm and deep to shallow and scattered. Her head begins to sway from side to side while she begins to perspire. Emmett, who had just returned after killing Pierre, walks into the main living room, infuriated, dejected, and in unbearable emotional pain.

It is pouring down outside, and Emmett is soaked to the bone. He gazes out the window, unsure of what to do with himself.

Emmett refuses to acknowledge Helena. His back faces her as she addresses him.

"Emmett," Helena says tearfully.

He doesn't respond. The water drips from his clothes and onto the floor. Helena stays where she is, preferring to keep her distance. She is unsure of what he may do to her if she comes too close.

"Emmett, please say something," she tries again in almost a whisper. But still, she gets no response.

He pushes his sopping black hair away from his face as the tears fall from his fervent gaze. Observing as the rain cascades from the sky, he wishes his reality was completely different. Emmett does not want to be here; the whole situation feels like a nightmare.

Part of him blames Helena for ruining him. He was once a man of high moral ethics, but this person he has become is one he does not wish to know.

The desires and strength of feelings she can bring forth in him frighten Emmett.

"Emmett," Helena says as her body trembles in fear at her husband's silence. "What happened?" She gets a little bit closer to Emmett, trying to encourage a response. "What did you do?"

Her questioning makes his body visibly tense as his right-hand balls up in a tight fist. And finally prompts a response.

"What did I do?" he snarls, spinning to face her. "More like what did you do?"

"I know, what I did was wrong. But going after Pierre is not going to fix anything," she answers him, weeping.

Emmett shakes his head in disbelief. "Even in death, you still defend him," he mutters with a sneer.

His words stop Helena from getting any closer.

"What do you mean by that?" she whispers.

Emmett glares at Helena from where he stands, his tall and muscular frame even more apparent as the wet clothes stick to his body like a second skin.

"Did I ever have you completely?" Emmett demands.

"Answer me," Helena pleads. "What did you do?"

"What was I to you? A second choice that you were happy to settle for?" he continues.

Helena shakes her head, as she cries remorsefully.

"If you truly loved me, you would not have done this! You would not have hurt me this way!" he shouts.

"I *do* love you," Helena says faintly.

Emmett shakes his head, sending water droplets to the floor from his drenched hair. "No. I loved you. I gave you everything. I gave you my all, and you betray me in return."

He stalks over to rest his hand on the fireplace mantel, completely grim.

"I will never forgive you," he mutters.

His blue eyes fixate on the fire before him. The reflection of the flames in his eyes perfectly reflects how he feels on the inside. Writhing in emotional pain the tears begin to well they feel hot against his cool damp skin.

"But despite it all, I still love you," Emmett hisses.

Emmett brings his hands to his face and covers his eyes as he cries, completely broken by Helena's betrayal. There are no words to describe the pain he feels, after the love of his life has betrayed him in a such a careless manner.

Helena sits on the sofa as far away from Emmett as she can and musters the courage to ask once more.

"You still have not answered me," she begins while her voice shakes. "What did you mean by your previous statement?"

Emmett coldly stares at his wife for a moment before answering. After his last few words, his unanswered question is what she wants to know the most. Making him feel that he is correct in suspecting that she did not love him as deeply as he loves her, all she cares about is Pierre in that moment.

After everything that has transpired, that is what she is most concerned about.

His cold stare turns into a menacing one as he suddenly douses out the fire, startling her.

"He's dead," he says vengefully. "I killed him."

Helena rises from her seat in horror. "What—"

She struggles to speak, her chest heaving for air. She can't believe the words coming out of Emmett's mouth.

He walks up to Helena slowly and coldly, observing her reaction to the news. The horror in her eyes makes him feel twistedly delighted.

"I walked right into his home and killed him. He's dead."

A sob wrenches from Helena's throat, and she tries to get away from Emmett but fails as he grips her body and pulls her towards him by her arms.

"What did you think was going to happen, darling?" he taunts.

"Let me go!" Helena shouts. "You are a monster!"

Emmett shoves Helena back onto the sofa with great force.

He hovers closely over her mortified face. His malevolent stare sends chills all over Helena's body.

"I am what you made me," he sneers.

He leaves Helena on the sofa, alone. Emmett takes a full bottle of brandy up to their bathroom and runs himself a hot bath.

He proceeds to drown himself in alcohol for days.

Suffice to say, he looks dreadful, unlike the dashing and composed man he typically is. Helena and Emmett go a week without speaking to one another despite living under the same roof.

Emmett from that lifetime would go on to carry with him karmic issues such as fear of loss, struggles of attachment, jealousy, possessiveness, control, and manipulation, as well as paranoia, most specifically in his intimate love relationships.

As for Helena, guilt, indecisiveness, and the inability to trust herself plague her in future incarnations.

The deeds sown in that lifetime would go on to haunt them.

As Rose relives those moments, she sees traces of the past in her present. Yet as painful as the past is, it gives her great clarity for her present.

Back in the past, fearing that he could face the gallows and social scandal, Emmett packs up the family and decides to settle elsewhere. Despite his family's connections, he knows it may not be enough to spare him.

One night as Helena returns from a trip to town, she finds her husband and their children waiting for her in the living room. She can see from Emmett's appearance that he has not slept in days.

"What is going on?" Helena asks carefully, setting down her things.

"We are leaving," Emmett answers, voice cold. "It's only a matter of time before they come for me."

Helena removes her gloves and throws them on the table before her. "So, we flee?"

Emmett nods.

"That's the solution? And what? Forget everything?!" Helena begins to cry.

Their housekeeper takes the children out to the garden to give them room to talk.

"You want to go on as if nothing happened?" Helena whispers in horror.

Emmett tries to approach slowly.

"Don't," she snaps, wiping her tears away. "I suppose I don't have a choice in the matter, do I? You've already decided for all of us, it looks like."

"Would you rather stay here and face whatever may come?" Emmett challenges.

"All I can think of is our children. What life will they have if we stay?" Helena cries, heartbroken.

Emmett nods in agreement. "My family owns an island not too far from here, but far enough to where they won't find us. We can start over there."

Helena looks down at her feet angrily. "Like I said, it's not as if I have a choice." She walks up to Emmett and glares at him. "I know what I did was wrong, and I'm sorry. But why don't you just throw me over your shoulder, and do as you wish while you are at it?"

She shuffles around in agony over the situation.

"Not as if my opinion matters to you," Helena mutters.

Emmett shakes his head in disbelief. "Don't act like you never had a choice in this! You chose to have an affair. Take responsibility for that!" he shouts.

"That's the thing, you always make me think I have a choice in the matter, but I don't. You coerce and manipulate me so you can get your way," Helena retorts hotly.

Emmett signals his coachmen waiting near the front door to load the last of the luggage onto the carriage. Helena quickly tries to run up the steps to their room, but Emmett grabs her before she can ascend the first few steps.

"Fine," he says and throws her over his shoulder. As she struggles to break free, he stalks outside to where the carriage will take them to their new home.

"Let go of me!" she yells, hitting him to make him put her down.

And he does, but only to shove her through the carriage doors. "Don't bother fighting this. Welcome to your new life, Helena."

Chapter 13

The home on the island turns out to be grand and spacious, proving to be a day's boat ride from England. The grounds are beautiful and peaceful, and maybe this won't be so utterly terrible.

Slowly, they do their best to rebuild their lives. But the guilt Helena feels will never let her know peace again. Months go by, and Helena tries to slowly rekindle intimacy between herself and Emmett, but he won't touch her.

What is certain is that a ghost follows them wherever they go. One they cannot escape.

Victoria's voice counts down. "Five, four, three, two, one."

Rose opens her eyes, her breath catching at the sight of the present world. She lies there for a second. "I know where the home is," she says to Victoria. "Ellum Island, it's called."

"The home?" Victoria asks, distracted as she jots down her notes.

"Yes, the home Emmett and Helena lived out their lives in after... the incident."

Victoria looks at Rose curiously. "Would you like to go see it?" she asks Rose.

A puzzled expression appears on Rose's face.

"I know where it is," Victoria explains, glancing down at

her notes in her lap. "The home is still owned by our family, you see. It isn't far from here."

Rose watches as Victoria's eyes fill with tears for the first time.

"Rose, you understand the severity of the situation, don't you? After what we both have now seen, if you and Emery can't break out of the karmic cycle you are in…"

Rose remembers her earlier session with Victoria and nods stoically.

"There is still hope that you can change it. You both can. The future is not set in stone. It never is." Victoria wipes away a tear and pulls herself together. "You and Emery can go as soon as possible. There is no time to waste."

Rose's brows raise. "Won't you come with us?" she asks. "We could use your gifts as we explore the place."

Victoria smiles. "If you wish."

After her session with Victoria, Rose spends most of her time in the rose garden alone, enjoying the sunny day before it goes away. She lies on the grass amongst the flowers and admires the blue sky above her.

Her body enveloped in a cream linen dress with roses imprinted upon it, fits her surroundings perfectly. Rose can feel the fear rising in her chest while she remembers the future probability she had seen.

Although she had chosen Emery, wholeheartedly, part of her still wants to run away from him. Maybe if she leaves Emery, things would be easier, she thinks, and the future wouldn't seem so bleak.

But there are no guarantees, and that scares her. In the end, she can only control herself.

Emery and Sir Ashby finally arrive as the sun begins to set. Rose stays where she is as Emery comes out to find her. He kneels beside her on the grass and let's himself go, completely melting into Rose's embrace.

It is the longest they have been away from one another. Although Emery's mind was with Rose when they were apart, he hates being physically away from her.

"I missed you," Emery whispers, holding her tighter.

"I missed you too," Rose says, kissing him before he sits up.

She admires him as he plucks a rose off the nearest bush. He lays the flower on her chest and makes himself comfortable beside her.

"I have to tell you something," she says carefully.

Emery turns to look at Rose.

"I had another regression today with your mother, and we know where the home is. The home where we lived out our lives after everything happened."

Emery sits up. "Where is it?" he asks eagerly.

"The home is not too far from here. Your mother can give us specifics. Victoria said it is still owned by your family, and she has agreed to come with us."

"Alright, well, when can we go see it?"

"I'm assuming anytime we want. Tomorrow, maybe?" Rose says.

Emery nods and hurriedly gets up. "Come on, let's go make arrangements."

Rose follows Emery in a haste.

Victoria is sitting in her husband's study alongside him. They've been catching up after their time spent away from one another. Sir Ashby sees Emery and Rose at the door and rises from his seat to greet them.

"Come in, you two," he says warmly.

"I told him what I had seen," Rose tells Victoria. "I told him about the house."

She nods. "Oh, yes."

"When can we go see it?" Emery asks his mother intrigued. "The house my past-self ran off to?"

"Immediately, if you wish," Victoria answers earnestly.

Emery raises his brows, surprised by her response. "Really? I mean, I'm excited to see it, but it can wait a day or two." He shrugs.

"No, it's best to uncover as much as you can. It's in your best interest to do so."

Emery picks up on his mother's seriousness and can't help but think that what Rose and his mother have seen is dire.

"Alright, if you say so," Emery says, a little uneasy. "How do we get there?"

Victoria rises from her seat and kisses Sir Ashby goodbye. "I will see you in three days," she whispers. "We can take the plane there," Victoria answers her son. "Come on," she says to both Emery and Rose.

Like eager and excited children, they both follow her.

⋅⧼⟐⧽⋅

The flight to the island only takes thirty minutes. Rose and Emery look out their windows, trying to catch a glimpse of anything. They can see a manor and a few houses spread out; the island is well lit with trees draped in landscaping lights.

"I've never been here," Emery admits to his mother.

She shakes her head. "No, we don't come here often. The estate is used mostly for other things, like private events. It's all business."

"Did you know about me?" Emery asks. "About my soul? The moment of my birth?"

Victoria smiles, but it's bittersweet. "Yes, I did."

"Then you must've known what I did and the house… all of this," Emery says.

"Yes and no. Information comes in on a need-to-know basis," Victoria tells her son.

"And I needed to know this?" He raises a brow.

Victoria nods. "Yes." She clears her throat and tries to control her emotions as she looks at Emery. "I am here to act as your guide in the flesh and help you two sort your karmic work out."

Rose turns to look at Victoria. "This was all pre-destined..." she whispers, bewildered.

"That's the greatest secret: Everything is," Victoria remarks. "But there are loopholes. Your souls chose one another before you came into this physical plane. I am sure I don't need to tell you this as you both already know, but you are true soulmates.

"The others are karmic mates, meant to teach you lessons for a while. But not meant to last."

Emery's blue eyes light up. "Did you know exactly how this was going to play out?"

"What, exactly?" Victoria tilts her head.

"How Rose and I met," Emery elaborates.

"Like I said, there are loopholes." She shrugs. "Some things are clear if you are decided on a certain action. But if you change your mind and make a different decision then the future or outcome changes, in that instance. I can see what is most likely to happen."

"So, we still have some control?" he presses.

"Well, on certain things. On you two meeting? No. That was going to happen regardless," Victoria adds. "But let's say I tell you something that is crucial to Fate's design," she says. "Your chances of changing it are higher. You have heard the old saying, you create your reality?"

"Yes," Emery says with a nod.

"Well..." Victoria says, shrugging. "Take this all with a

grain of salt. Because even the universe and higher realms keep me in the dark. You think something is one way and it ends up being another."

"It must be maddening!" Emery exclaims.

"Oh, yes," Victoria laughs. "But I think your case is peculiar. There is room for change in the outcome because the good outcome boils down solely to whether you can evolve and outgrow your old relational patterns."

Emery raises a brow at his mother. "How so?" he asks.

She smirks. "Are you really going to pretend that you don't feel jealous over Rose? Your need for control? Even now? The emotional outbursts you have and the ones most likely yet to be are not exactly under your control I dare say."

Chapter 14

They land on Ellum Island a few minutes later, much to Emery's relief. The landing strip was slightly difficult to see because of the temporary fog that sat in a thick haze over the island. Their pilot had to circle around twice before finally deeming it safe.

Their driver picks them up from the airport and promptly takes them to where they are staying. Victoria guides them throughout the property, but Rose explores the home as if she knows it like the back of her hand.

"I can't help but feel sad," Rose tells Victoria while she admires the interior of the home.

"It's probably your soul remembering its time here."

Emery helps brings the bags into the area they are standing in.

"How are you feeling?" Victoria asks her son. "Are you picking up anything?"

Emery glances around. "Should I?" He cocks an eyebrow.

"This is where you both lived out your lives in your past life. I figured that perhaps you would."

Emery shakes his head. "Not feeling anything."

"Well, maybe you could do a regression and see if that makes a difference. Rose is the one who was able to see the home most recently."

"Alright," Emery says.

Victoria shows them where they will be staying. The home has been well-kept for many generations. It is primarily used for hosting private events, but the family did their best to keep many of the original designs and furnishings.

Rose picks up on the home's energy far easier than Emery. A sad haunting sensation lingers around her. Walking into that house makes her feel as if she has stepped back in time.

A nostalgia her rational mind can't quite grasp engulfs her. They have recovered some of their old belongings by sheer coincidence on Emery's behalf; they found the old wooden box containing Emmett's old gun and the miniature portrait of Helena at the old, abandoned estate near the Williams home.

Rose can't help but wonder if the ring is still possibly lost somewhere. She truly hopes that they can find it. She thinks that if anyone would know where it is, it would be Helena.

Maybe it was buried with her? Rose thinks to herself. That's the most probable answer.

Everyone settles into their rooms to rest. Rose lies beside Emery and snuggles up to him. He doesn't waste much time before passionately kissing her.

His hands glide down her body to remove her underwear, but she isn't wearing any under her night slip, a fact which brings a coy smile to his lips. Rose smirks and positions herself underneath Emery's body.

His lips meet hers fervently, and their breathing becomes heavier as his fingers enter her ever so slowly. Rose moans, and her delicate hands grip the nape of Emery's neck, pulling him closer.

He continues kissing her as his fingers stimulate her further. Not wanting to wait any longer, Rose grips Emery's penis and guides it into her wet and aroused vagina.

As it gently glides in, Emery's lips caress hers, and the explosion of pleasure that they make each other feel is formidable. He breathlessly bites her neck as he thrusts harder, while Rose's hands are interlocked in Emery's thick dark hair.

She moans louder as she gets closer to climaxing. Emery's hands grip Rose firmly as he finishes inside her. Both of their bodies are pulsing with euphoria. He rests his head on her chest as he catches his breath, and they both hold one another in silence.

Every time they have sex, it becomes increasingly intense. Their souls belong to one another; and just being together brings them both great fulfillment, despite the struggles they endure individually due to their past wounds.

Satiated, they both fall fast asleep in each other's embrace.

The following morning, Victoria is downstairs in the kitchen with the kitchen staff, preparing breakfast. The sun is rising, and Rose makes her way down the wooden stairs quietly. Emery is still sleeping in their bed.

"Good morning," Rose whispers to Victoria as she enters the kitchen area.

"Good morning," Victoria says back softly. "You're up early."

"Yes. I feel well-rested." Rose smiles, helping herself to a cup of coffee from the breakfast spread before her.

"What should we explore today?" Victoria asks inquisitively, pursing her lips.

Rose finishes gulping down some of her coffee before she answers. She sits down in the cozy breakfast nook overlooking the sunrise.

"I don't know. I suppose we could just walk around and photograph the place. I brought my camera," she suggests.

"Okay, I'm thinking Emery is due for another regression.

Perhaps tonight we can plan for that," Victoria adds. She's been picking at the croissant in front of her for a good few seconds.

"Do you not like it?" Rose asks, chuckling.

Victoria's large blue eyes widen as she looks at Rose. "Oh, I do. I just have been rather pensive this morning. I'm worried about Emery."

"How so?" Rose asks, her brows pushing together with concern.

"Well, it may not be manifesting now, but it is a sure probability that he could struggle to heal his wounds from the past during this life cycle."

Victoria spins her little silver spoon in her coffee.

"You both are being gifted an opportunity to get this right. If he can't heal, the relationship will turn toxic, and it will end. I know that is the worst-case scenario for you both, but most specifically it is for Emery. He won't fare well if he loses you."

Victoria suddenly stops talking as she hears steps behind her. Emery has awoken. He steers himself directly towards the breakfast buffet before joining them.

"Good morning," Victoria says to her son. "Did you sleep well?"

"Excellent!" Emery answers with a smile. He shoves half a croissant in his mouth, hardly chewing as it disappears.

"Someone's famished," Victoria mutters.

Emery sits right beside Rose and rests a very territorial hand on her thigh.

"I was suggesting to Rose that you should probably have a regression session tonight. Just you. What do you think?" Victoria suggests to Emery, who is still eating the remainder of his croissant.

He nods in agreement without being able to talk as he chews. The crumbs messily fall onto his lap.

"We can walk around the grounds here," she continues. "I don't know what else remains from the past besides this main house and the furniture in it. But the grounds on the island are rather impressive."

"I think a nice walk around the island would be phenomenal," Emery finally answers after swallowing.

The island is stunning, with little beaches around the area and some cliffsides overlooking the vast ocean. Rose can see why the island was the perfect place for them to run to in the past.

It is peaceful, but the tragedy they left behind was not. Hand in hand, Rose and Emery walk around with Victoria as she shares the information she receives from the guides on the other side.

They give Victoria little details about moments Helena and Emmett had here and how hard Emmett struggled to forgive Helena. Her betrayal destroyed him in that life, and he was never the same; the guides express to Victoria how even in the present life Emery, Emmett's present-self, fears his great love betraying him again.

Those fears are tied to the past betrayal, the brutal pain he endured then which he still carries in his soul. Manifesting in ways that are challenging to his present relationship.

Rose takes as many photographs as she can. Catherine would be interested in seeing them when they get back to Carmel. In one of the storage houses, Victoria leads them to an old carriage that was left behind by Helena and Emmett. Rose silently observes the carriage as chills run through her body.

It is the same carriage she has seen in her regressions. She just knows it, although obviously it's worn and old, but otherwise, it is as she remembers it.

"This is a marvelous find," Rose murmurs as she photographs it.

Emery opens the door of the carriage and eagerly steps inside.

"Be careful," Victoria warns. "It is very old; we don't want to break it."

"Alright," Emery replies, stepping back out of it quickly. "We need to protect this and make sure we can display it in an exhibit. We can show this to the world once we have found enough evidence of our existence in the past."

"I would be careful about that." Victoria frowns.

"Why?" Rose asks, turning to face her as she lowers her camera.

"Well, Emmett committed a crime. Although it occurred years ago, it still took place; you just never know what could happen. We don't want any negative attention."

"Oh, God. What are they going to do? Punish me? That would be like punishing a ghost," Emery laughs.

Victoria shrugs. "The choice is up to you two."

"I wouldn't mind sharing our findings with the world. It would be revolutionary," Rose adds. "I think the world needs to see this."

"It is very provocative," Emery agrees. "This proves that we continue to live, and we never truly die."

They slowly make their way down to the docks. The sand is soft and clear, and the freezing water is a sight to behold.

"Not a bad place to run away to," Rose remarks to Emery.

He stands beside her and smiles. His gaze observes Rose with fascination.

"Can you believe this?" he asks. "All this that we are discovering isn't just a big deal for us, but for the world. We get to answer the age-old question, *what more is there to life after death?*"

Rose nods. "Absolutely."

"This is the best archeological find of my career," Emery says excitedly.

"Do you think Emmett and Helena were buried on this island?" Rose asks him.

Before he can answer, Victoria does.

"Yes, they were, and I believe they still are. There is a mausoleum on the island. We can go there."

Eager to see where Helena and Emmett were laid to rest, Rose wastes no time and encourages Victoria and Emery to go immediately. As they approach the mausoleum, Rose can see the Williams name etched into the top of the entrance.

An unpleasant shiver courses through her, making her shudder. Emery follows slowly behind her.

The grey and dark stones of the mausoleum are covered in dust and overgrown ivy; no one has really touched the place or visited by the looks of it. Rose follows the dark and musty hallway down to Helena's resting place. By the dates on the stone, she discovers that Helena died before Emmett at eighty-years old.

She dusts off some of the cobwebs, uncovering the engraved message on the tomb. *"Not even in death will our souls be parted. We will find one another again and begin anew. Our love is eternal and unwavering, like the tides of the sea. I will meet you there." -E*

Rose reads it to herself in a faint whisper.

"A true poet, until the end," she says aloud to Victoria and Emery. "Emmett wrote this. Look, the E at the end." Rose thinks quickly. "What came to mind immediately was—"

"Carmel by-the-sea," Victoria interjects before Rose can finish speaking. "You're correct. By Fate's design, you met by the tides of the sea…" A soft smile spreads over her face

The synchronicities reveal themselves like a wink from the universe. Just as she had seen in her visions.

"Your love story was far from over," she says to both Emery and Rose.

But Emery's gaze is still fixed on the words carved into the stone.

"Almost as if I set the intention and here we are, once more manifested in the flesh."

Rose smiles wondrously. She pulls out her camera and photographs the entire area.

"Catherine is going to love seeing this!" she beams.

"Do you think Helena was buried with the emerald ring?" Emery asks his mother.

"I have tried to gain knowledge on it from the guides, but they haven't shown me any concrete leads," Victoria tells him with a frown. "It would be the most incredible find, if I do say so myself."

"Oh, absolutely!" Emery adds. "We must find it!"

"It had to stay in the family perhaps, if it isn't buried with Helena," Rose chimes.

"Who knows?" Victoria whispers as she thinks long and hard about where it could possibly be.

"Do you think we could open the tomb and check to see if the ring is in here with her?" Emery asks.

Victoria's eyes widen. "I don't know. Do you think that would be a good idea?"

"Isn't that disrespectful?" Rose shifts uncomfortably.

Emery turns to look at her. "I do this kind of stuff for a living. We open tombs in Egypt holding dead pharaohs. I'm sure it will be fine," he says, waving her off.

"Yes, but won't we get in trouble? I hate to point out the obvious, but isn't it frowned upon?"

"Well, we want to find this thing, don't we?" Emery insists.

Rose hesitantly nods.

"Let's wait a little more; maybe it could be at the old abandoned estate where you found the wooden box?" Victoria suggests.

Chapter 15

B ack at the main house, they have a late lunch and rest for a while. Rose journals her findings and leaves Emery with his mother in the library.

"We can start now with a regression if you'd like?" Victoria tells Emery as she sits by the lit fireplace. Its flickering embers cast amber hues over her face. "We can discover the rest of the story."

Emery nods and rests on the sofa. "Hopefully, we can try and find the location of the ring," he suggests.

"Let's see if we can recover some helpful memories to point us in the right direction," Victoria says with a nod.

"That would be lovely."

She begins counting him down into a deep hypnosis state. He is immediately brought into a scene with Helena as Emmett.

They are there on the island, living with their children and the remaining household staff that came with them when they fled. Helena is trying to make love to him for the first time since the tragedy unfolded. But he can't bring himself to touch her; he is disgusted by the fact that another man has sullied her body.

Every time he remembers her ruthless betrayal, he can't help but reject her. Yet at the same time, he wants her so badly.

He pushes her away from him and flees from her. He then

drowns himself in liquor and stays in the library, lamenting his sorrows. Helena stays in her bedroom alone, saddened that they can't make any progress.

She knows she doesn't deserve Emmett's forgiveness, but she wishes they could move forward.

Later that night, he drunkenly barges into the master bedroom where Helena lies asleep. As he stumbles onto the bed, he jolts her awake.

"What are you doing?" Helena says, alarmed by his sudden appearance.

Emmett doesn't answer; he simply grabs her and begins undressing her. Helena can smell the liquor on his breath and can tell he has been brooding in the library all night.

Emmett kisses Helena for the first time since her affair. He takes her that night without permission. Emmett's manner of initiating was always the same: He would spend time holding her and caressing Helena before ever trying to be intimate with her. But not this time.

However, she doesn't fight him and kisses him back. She welcomes his advances, hoping they can move forward. His lovemaking is rough and aggressive, unlike before.

Emmett is conflicted in his emotions for his wife. He makes himself at home in between her thighs as he makes her his again. His lips fervently brush up against her neck.

Emery can see that he was completely heartbroken in that lifetime as Emmett.

"I have to heal this heartbreak," Emery says softly aloud while under hypnosis. "And the way to do that is by loving her again and forgiving her."

"Can you do it?" Victoria asks her son, her voice quiet in the trance.

Emery struggles. He fears that if he forgives her, she will

take him for granted and betray him again. The heaviness in his heart won't allow him to be at peace.

When he tries to relax, the pain resurfaces. He knows his paranoia and jealousy is not healthy, but he can't help it. The underlying terror that the past will repeat itself is there. It causes him to fear losing Rose to Phillip; the thought alone is torture.

"His emotions are so strong. Emmett's hurt is hard to get past. That part of me can't let go. It is scared that she will betray me again."

"Understandable," Victoria says.

"There is fear over her loss in whatever form that may be. But fear of loss is there. She died before me; I was devastated by her death. I was miserable for the remainder of my years," Emery says as he watches the scenes before him.

He continues.

"Emmett's hurt also stems from how she let herself go with Pierre, how easily she was swayed to sleep with him and rekindle that past love instead of remaining loyal to him. He could never do that to her."

Emery begins to be shown the day of Helena's burial.

"She wasn't buried with the ring," he relays to his mother. "It stayed in the family; they stored it under total secrecy in a vault."

Victoria leans forward, her attention piqued. "Do you know where it could be roughly?" she asks eagerly.

Emery shakes his head. "I can't make it out. But it looks like England."

Victoria thinks to herself if it could possibly be amongst the family jewels. But it can't be she would've seen it.

She guides Emery towards the end of his life in the regression and brings him back, except before she counts down to three, the ascended masters speak to her through Emery.

These ascended masters are different to his usual guides, as they carry more authority over universal laws and souls' experiences on Earth.

They watch over him to see if he will pass his karmic lesson; what he did in the past is a serious violation of universal law. He robbed another soul of their free will to choose.

His soul carries the punishment for his wrongful deeds through his paranoia, jealousy, and inability to be at peace. His opportunity to incarnate again and make things right is his mercy granted by the ascended masters.

"The lesson here is for him to let go and forgive. Control is fear, while love is freedom. If she decides to leave him, he must let her go. Letting go is the ultimate expression of love," Gabriel, the ascended master, shares.

After a few seconds, Emery opens his eyes as he slowly comes back to his present consciousness, glancing around the library.

Victoria looks at her son and smiles. She doesn't tell him just yet what occurred; she holds off until tomorrow. "Get some rest," she says and excuses herself to her bedroom.

Emery rushes back to Rose. He opens the bedroom door and sees she has fallen asleep, on the bed, pen still in hand.

He kisses her neck, shaking her gently.

"Wake up," he whispers into her ear. His hands caress her body in a tender manner. "Wake up," he says again, his lips pressing against hers.

Her hazel eyes are now wide-open, and Rose kisses Emery back, running her fingers through his disheveled hair and gripping it tightly enough to playfully tug. Emery bites Rose's lips in retaliation.

She positions herself on top of his body, dominating him completely. He lets her have her way with him, and she unbuttons his pants and positions herself as he slips into her.

"I love you," Emery says to her breathlessly.

Rose slows down enough to answer him. She peers into his gaze that has haunted her for lifetimes. She would recognize his eyes anywhere, a look so uniquely impressed into her memory. Time itself could not erase it.

"I love you too," she whispers. Her hands rest on his shoulders as they admire one another.

Rose continues for a few minutes longer until they finish together. Emery stays inside of her afterward, paralyzed with satisfaction, his grip locked around Rose's backside.

"This is insane," Emery says in disbelief as pure ecstasy rolls through him.

Rose smirks, still locked on top of his body.

"I was wondering if it felt the same for you as it does for me," she admits.

"Intensely pleasurable? Euphoric?" Emery asks, smiling.

"Yes," Rose whispers.

He carefully pulls out of her and allows her to lie beside him. "It must be all those lifetimes together under our belt," he suggests. "Isn't it?"

Rose caresses Emery. "It must be. They say energy between souls builds over time."

"That would explain the intoxicating chemistry between us," Emery agrees, nodding off to sleep.

Rose rests her head on his chest, his heartbeat resounding gracefully in her ear, a sweet symphony that grounds her in his arms.

"I love you," she whispers in his ear and drifts off to sleep, too.

Their visit on the island comes to an end the following morning. There wasn't much else to see, and Emery's grandfather had sent word that he wanted to see Emery before he returned to his home in London.

As they arrive back at The Williams Estate, Emery looks for his grandfather to see what he wishes to speak to him about. He finds him sitting with his father in the study amidst conversation.

"Oh, good, you're back," his grandfather says, offering him a delighted smile.

Emery walks in, intrigued. "My mother said you wanted to speak to me about something?"

"I'll leave you two," Sir Ashby says, eager to greet his wife.

Emery's grandfather nods. "Can you close the door behind you?" he asks Sir Ashby.

"Yes, of course." With a nod farewell, he departs the room.

Emery's interest is piqued further. "What's going on? What is this about?" he presses, dying to know.

His grandfather smiles as he sits in his leather tufted chair. "Well, I was thinking the other night as I was talking to your father. He mentioned to me that you are very serious about this young lady and that you plan to marry her."

"Yes, that's right." Emery nods.

"In that case," his grandfather trails off.

He reaches his hand behind him and pulls out a little black velvet bag. His grandfather loosens the top tie to reveal a small red box before placing it in Emery's hand.

"Would you like to use this ring to give her?" Emery's grandfather asks proudly.

Emery opens the box and can't believe his eyes.

"Oh my God!" he blurts out.

In the box is a magnificently cut emerald set on a dainty golden band. The very same ring they had all been searching for is finally in his hands.

"Where did you get this?" Emery asks his grandfather, his voice barely above a whisper.

"It has been in the family for centuries. No one knows we have it; there are people searching for it. We have protected it by keeping its existence in our vault a secret."

His grandfather pours himself and Emery a glass of brandy to celebrate.

"Are you familiar with this ring?" he asks Emery, glancing over at him.

"I had heard about it from my friend Theodore. He's searching for this ring."

Emery's grandfather raises his brows.

"I bet he does. He isn't the only one, of course. The band is made of pure gold and is very malleable. So, it must be protected and worn carefully. The emerald is incredibly rare; our ancestor Emmett Williams came to possess this stone. King George IV of England gifted it to him. After they traveled together through the emerald mines, looking for precious stones for the king, Emmett found it, and the king graciously decided to let him keep it.

"The Williams family has been in the banking business for a long time, but we have also ventured into other types of business, such as mining precious stones like this one."

Emery takes the glass of brandy from his grandfather excitedly. "My mother didn't even know you had it."

"No, like I said, it was best to keep it a secret. Until now, it is a good fit for you as the only heir of the family. The ring also has quite the dark history."

"How so?" Emery asks.

His grandfather sits down beside him and looks down at his feet, his shoulders tense as he lets out a sigh. Bracing himself for what he is about to divulge.

"Our ancestor Emmett Williams was madly in love with his wife, Helena. But she was unfaithful with a past lover from her native country Spain, and Emmett killed him."

Emery almost spits out his drink. He is absolutely gob smacked.

All of it is true. The regressions both he and Rose have been seeing are all the absolute truth.

"What else?" Emery presses, eager to learn more.

"Well, as the story goes, the man she had an affair with was French, but he migrated to Spain to work for Helena's father. When her father found out that they were romantically involved, he sent her away to live with our family. That is how Emmett Williams came to meet his wife."

His grandfather pauses, thinking quietly.

"Emmett James was the last name he was known by then. He changed it to Williams after he committed murder, and we have been using it ever since to hide the dark past of this family."

Chapter 16

"Let's just say it wasn't a very happy ending. They left chaos in their wake, and they fled to a nearby island," his grandfather continues, pausing again as he does his best to remember the details. "Why, I believe it is the island that all of you just came back from."

"Oh, yes. My mother showed us the grounds and the mausoleum. Both Emmett James and Helena are buried there," Emery says in amazement.

"Wow! Well, it isn't something we like to discuss in the family, as you understand; it isn't something to be proud of. "But being that you are the only heir in the family, it seems fit that you should have it to give to Rose. I think she'd be speechless upon seeing it!"

Emery looks at the ring sitting in the box in his hand. It is incredibly beautiful and rich in color. The gold band suits the emerald color of the stone immaculately.

"Yes, she will indeed," Emery agrees, smiling from ear to ear. "I can't wait to present it to her."

Emery's grandfather hugs him and congratulates him on the incredible milestone he is about to embark on.

"When do you plan on proposing to Rose?" he asks.

"As soon as possible," Emery answers excitedly. "I just want her to be my wife already."

His grandfather pulls out of the little bag some old parchment paper. "This is the authentic paperwork for the ring." He unfolds the paper. "Look here."

He points at a very large and elegant signature that reads, *Emmett James.*

"My God!" Emery blurts out. "This is incredible. Thank you so much!"

"Take care of it. It is an invaluable piece of family history, no matter how tainted it may be."

Emery nods and places all the items back in the little bag. "I will have to propose to her soon. I don't think I can keep this a secret for long."

"Will you propose while I'm here?"

"Tomorrow, I have something in mind," Emery says adamantly. "I will ask her to marry me tomorrow. I want to share this with all of you. Everything must be perfect."

"Very well, my boy." His grandfather grins.

Emery wraps him in a tight hug, beaming with joy.

Bidding his grandfather farewell, Emery runs up the stairs to hide the ring in his room where Rose won't accidentally find it.

He racks his brain trying to decide how to ask Rose to marry him. He thinks the rose garden would be the best option. He excitedly plots how he will execute his vision.

After successfully hiding the ring, Emery joins his family in the garden. A great big smile adorns his face, raising suspicions on behalf of his mother and Rose.

"Aren't you happy?" his mother comments, raising a curious brow.

Emery nods. "Oh, you have no idea," he answers.

He briskly walks up to his mother and pulls her away from the group. He interlocks his arm with hers and guides her towards the pond where the swans drift over the water.

"You won't believe what grandfather just gave me," Emery whispers.

Victoria turns to look at him. "And what is that?"

"The ring we have all been looking for," he excitedly answers.

She lets go of his arm in shock. "Really?!"

"Yes." He nods.

His mother places her hands on the sides of her face as she lets out a squeal.

"I am going to propose to Rose tomorrow."

Victoria nods. "Good, I can start to quietly plan the engagement party." A giant smile adorns her face.

"If you wish, yes."

She smiles. "Of course. Everyone must meet her; she will be formally introduced as the new member of the family, after all."

At dinner, Emery is acting different. Rose can sense that something has happened, but she isn't quite sure what. He is exceptionally amorous, far more than usual.

"How was your time on the island?" Alice asks Emery.

"It was nice; we discovered some new information about our ancestors," he says.

"Oh, we don't go very often. I was surprised you all felt the need to. We should visit more," Alice remarks, taking a bite of her meal.

Victoria nods. "It is lovely there. The views are splendid."

"Oh, yes. Yes, they are," Alice agrees.

"I think it would be a great location for a wedding, don't you think, Emery?" his grandfather suggests, taking a sip of water.

Emery smiles at him. "Possibly."

Rose glances at Emery and his grandfather, growing increasingly suspicious.

After dinner, Emery decides to play the piano for everyone. Sir Ashby brings out the best bottle of wine they have in the cellar.

"1981," Sir Ashby says proudly as he showcases the bottle to his father.

"Ooh, give it here," he quips, extending his glass out.

"I don't think you should be having any," Alice chides her husband. "You've already helped yourself to the brandy in the study. It isn't wise to mix drinks."

"We are celebrating," he protests whispering into his wife's ear.

He brings his finger up to his lips, signaling her to keep what he just told her to herself.

Emery plays a new song he has not played before. Victoria doesn't recognize the song and can only assume it is something new he has composed.

Rose watches Emery's fingers dance over the keys, bewitched.

The song is one he created specifically for Rose. Just like his mother had created one for him, he wanted to do something for her that was special and unique, just like her. It is timeless and profound, and everyone in the room watches him play attentively.

As the song comes to an end, it is late, and one by one people leave the living room, until only Rose and Emery are left.

"Did you like the song?" Emery asks Rose.

She hugs Emery and melts in his arms. "Yes, I did."

Emery kisses Rose ardently and rests his forehead on hers. "I wrote it for you."

Rose observes Emery. His gaze longingly observes her back.

"I have something planned for us tomorrow," he reveals.

Rose buries her face in Emery's neck. "What is it?"

Emery hugs her a little tighter. "You'll see."

"Let's go to bed," Rose whispers. "I'm tired."

Emery scoops up her in his arms and carries her off to the bedroom.

She squeals, kicking her feet. "What are you doing? Put me down."

Emery ignores her and carries on.

Chapter 17

They lie in bed snuggled up together, something Emery and Rose have grown accustomed to by now. All Emery can think about is how he is going to propose to Rose tomorrow.

"I love you," Emery says to her as they gaze into each other's eyes. "It is a miracle that we are here together again. After everything we have discovered."

Rose's lips meet his neck as he speaks. His tantalizing scent arouses her.

"Make love to me," she whispers in his ear. "As if this was our last night together."

Emery perks up at the sound of her request. "I thought you were tired?"

Rose smirks, and Emery obliges her request. His kisses become slower and deeper as he ever so slowly moves to his favorite place. His lips focus on her clitoris.

As he consumes her, his hands clasp onto her hips as Rose shifts under him. She can't help herself and begins to moan. Emery places his right hand on her mouth. The house is deathly quiet, and his parents' bedroom is across from theirs.

He positions his hips against hers and begins to thrust slowly, his wet lips carrying her scent on them. When Emery delicately bites her lips, Rose closes her eyes and enjoys the sensations he gifts her.

Emery passionately turns Rose around and continues thrusting from behind. His hands seize her body with power and need. She is completely subjugated to him.

As he goes deeper and deeper, she gasps. Emery explosively finishes inside of Rose while she orgasms. He delights in hearing her moan. He keeps her close to him as they rest. Emery kisses Rose fervidly; he can't get enough of her. Her taste on his lips is addictive.

He is intoxicated and bewitched by her—body, mind, and soul.

Rose falls asleep completely drunk from the pleasure she's experienced. Emery holds her in his arms, soaking in their love.

❦

As the sun rises the next morning, Emery sits up on his bed, naked. Rose is still asleep beside him. The day has come where he gets the extraordinary honor to ask her to marry him. It's all he can think about.

Emery freshens up, gets dressed, and heads downstairs. He walks to the pond on the property to enjoy the stillness of the morning. Victoria walks out to meet him as waves lap against the shore.

"So, what have you got in mind?" she asks inquisitively. "Will you propose in the morning, evening, or night?"

Emery turns to look at his mother as the breeze tangles in his hair. "I think around noon. In the rose garden."

"Do you want us to stay inside while you propose?"

"Yes, but don't make it obvious or anything," Emery says, looking at the water before him pensively. The sun gleams down over the rippling pond; it is a beautiful day, indeed. Perfect for what he has planned.

Victoria nods. "Alright."

Emery smiles, his face beaming like the sun.

Meanwhile, Rose awakens to find herself alone in bed. She lies there remembering the night before. Emery's tantalizing touch on her skin lingers.

She wishes he would make love to her again in that moment.

While she gets up to take a shower, Emery becomes increasingly nervous; he hasn't had any serious and formal conversations with Rose about marriage.

His proposal will be very much a surprise, but it seems the most natural step for them, considering how madly in love they are with one another. He can only hope she says yes. Taking a calming breath, Emery decides to meditate in the library alone to soothe his nerves.

If he does not keep his composure, Rose will sense something is in the works and the surprise will perhaps be spoiled.

When Rose comes down the steps dressed for the day, she wanders into the kitchen hoping to find Emery, but she finds Victoria instead. She is happily arranging rose bouquets; Rose counts roughly seventeen of them.

"What is the occasion?" Rose asks, pursing her lips at the sight.

Jolted, Victoria turns to look at Rose. "Oh!" she blurts out. "You scared me."

Rose smiles, abashed. "I'm sorry."

Victoria collects herself. "No occasion, just making some fresh arrangements. The old ones are starting to wilt."

Nannie arranges breakfast for Rose in the kitchen as they chat.

"Oh, you don't have to do that. I'll just have some coffee," Rose says to her.

"Coffee on an empty stomach is terrible. You must have something," Nannie scolds.

Rose obliges and takes a seat at the breakfast nook.

"Have you been sleeping all right?" Victoria inquires, making polite conversation.

Rose grins at her coffee while she remembers the night before with Emery. "Not quite."

Victoria glances over at her, confused. But Nannie blushes and carries on with her household duties. Had she heard them, Rose wonders? She flushes, digging into her food.

"It's probably the time change, I suppose," Victoria says, still clueless.

After eating, Rose strolls through the garden. The landscapers are trimming the tall bushes and crafting a maze design beside it.

"Would you like to enter?" the landscape designer asks her.

Rose looks at the entrance apprehensively. "Oh, I don't know."

"I'll accompany you," he chimes, leading the way in.

"It looks like something out of Alice in Wonderland," Rose tells him as she enters the tall green maze.

"That is what we were aiming for, a whimsical design." He nods.

"It's quite something," Rose remarks as she wanders around. The smell of freshly cut foliage engulfs her. The cool and shady atmosphere the maze provides is splendid.

"All the rain we get here makes this design possible."

"Oh, yes. I can see why; it keeps everything so green," Rose answers.

He guides her towards the end of the maze.

"Here we are," he says, leading the way out.

"This is fun. I'll have to show Emery when I find him."

"He actually hired me to do this."

"He did?" Rose asks, perturbed. "I'm sorry, what is your name? I'm Rose, by the way."

"George. Nice to meet you," he says, reaching out his hand to shake hers.

"Did he say why?" Rose says curiously.

George merely shrugs. "It's all done, if you'd like to take a look," he says abruptly to someone behind Rose. She spins around.

Emery stands behind them, dressed elegantly, as per usual.

"What is going on?" Rose asks him, narrowing her eyes in suspicion.

Emery grins, playing it cool.

"Thank you, George. It looks great," he answers, walking into the maze for himself. He extends his hand out to Rose. "Come with me?"

"Oh, I've already seen it," Rose says.

"But not with me." There's a twinkle to his eye she can't ignore.

Rose smiles and takes Emery's hand as the landscaper leaves. "Where have you been?" she whispers.

"I was meditating."

Without warning, Rose playfully takes off running before Emery through the maze.

Now out the other end, she waits for Emery to catch up, but he doesn't come out.

"Emery," Rose calls out to him.

She stands at the exit, peering into the shaded shrub maze, and doesn't hear a sound.

"Emery," she calls again, now growing impatient.

But he doesn't answer.

Rose mutters under her breath and walks back into the maze in search of him, finding him at the center of it.

He sits on the wooden bench, his eyes fixed on something in his right hand. Rose can't quite make out what it could be.

"Emery?" she murmurs, slowly approaching.

He looks up at her teary-eyed.

"Emery, what's wrong?" she asks, her voice laced with concern.

"Nothing," he answers, forcing a smile. "Everything is fine, but I would like for it to be perfect."

A puzzled expression forms on Rose's face.

Emery reveals the red box in his hand. All at once, the blood rushes from her face. Is he...?

Emery stands up from the bench and presents Rose with the emerald ring his grandfather gave him. The ring Emmett Williams had gifted his wife, Helena. The emerald serving as a symbol of his undying love, loyalty, and devotion to her.

A timeless promise not even death could break. To love her for eternity. As Emery opens the box, Rose gasps at the sight of the emerald, her hands flying to cover her mouth in surprise.

"I've thought of a few things to say to you, but words fail me. You have awakened emotions in me that I never thought I could feel. I love you with all that I am, in this life and the next. You are my wish fulfillment and more," Emery says nervously, his gaze intently watching Rose. "Will you marry me?" He kneels before her, waiting her answer.

Rose doesn't hesitate. "Yes," she says tearfully. "Yes!"

Emery carefully takes the ring out of the box and slowly puts it on Rose's ring finger. The weight of the ring on her hand is meaningful, and it suits her perfectly.

Emery pulls her body close to his, his delightful lips grace hers in a poetic manner. After all the time that has passed, their souls have found one another again and everything is as fate intended.

Without waiting another second, Rose undoes Emery's pants; she settles them on the grassy ground while she straddles him, her lips wildly meeting his in an intoxicating pull of lust and love. Emery's hand grips her neck, his mouth taking hold of her breast.

A soft gasp escapes her and lifting her dress to accommodate Emery's penis in her body, she takes him in deep.

Rose is hopelessly addicted to him. His touch ensnares her, leaving her helpless to resist. Gripping her firmly, Emery leaves a love bite on her breast. He positions himself atop her body, ferociously cradling her in his embrace.

As he drives his penis inside her, it isn't long before Rose feels the warm gush of Emery's come as they orgasm together.

His lips melt into hers seductively, intensifying her orgasm. Once the lust that clouded their heads like fog dissipates, Emery takes the words right out of Rose's mouth.

"Do you think anyone heard us?" he whispers.

She turns to look at him and smirks. "I don't know."

He brings Rose's hand up to his lips. The emerald ring is extravagant and hard not to admire. Tentatively, he presses a kiss to her skin.

"I meant to ask; did you have this made? Is it a replica of the original?" Rose asks him.

Emery shakes his head quickly. "No, baby, this is the real thing. My grandfather gave it to me yesterday when we returned from our trip."

Amazed, she admires it once more. "He had it all this time."

Emery rises from the grass and helps Rose up. As they begin to dress, he elaborates further.

"It was stored in the family vault under total secrecy. He

mentioned the history of the ring and spoke about Emmett and Helena," he adds, raising a brow and observing Rose's reaction to the information.

Pensively and astonished, Rose attempts to process what Emery is telling her. "So, it is true."

"That is exactly what I thought. We have more physical proof we existed in the past."

Rose stares out over the hedge maze, shaking her head in wonder. "This is... monumental."

Chapter 18

"Come, my mother must be waiting for us," Emery says, leading the way out of the tall hedge maze.

"She knew you were proposing?" Rose replies, her eyes widening.

"Sort of," he hesitates. "I let her know I would propose at noon. I wasn't sure if I was going to be able to pull it off though, is what I mean. It was a rough estimate."

Rose and Emery enter the living room area of the home where Victoria and Emery's grandmother Alice sit talking on the lounge chairs. They both glance up upon noticing their arrival.

"We have some news to share," Emery announces, grinning excitedly.

Both women turn their full attention to Rose and Emery, and the former sticks out her left hand to showcase the emerald ring on her finger.

"Oh my God!" Victoria blurts out. She rises from her seat quickly to look at the ring up close. "Is this…?" she asks Emery, her eyes shooting up to meet his.

He nods, confirming her suspicions. The ring is indeed the very same one from the past.

"Oh, congratulations!" Victoria hugs Rose, overjoyed, then her son. "Well, good, now I can get on with planning the engagement party out in the open."

Alice embraces Rose as well. "Welcome to the family," she

says softly with a warm smile. She turns to Emery. "Have you told your grandfather?"

"He knows I was going to ask her, but he doesn't know I already have. Where is he?"

She points towards the library. "Over there, I suppose, with your father. You know, those two are always attached at the hip."

Emery takes Rose's hand and walks them over to find his grandfather and Sir Ashby.

He opens the library door to reveal a billowing cloud of smoke.

"Oh, dear God!" Alice shouts, standing behind Rose. "You couldn't have the decency to smoke outside? Those nasty things!"

"I have news," Emery begins as he fans the smoke out of his face, walking into the room.

"Yes?" his grandfather replies, playfully fighting off Alice as she tries to wrestle the cigar from his mouth.

"I have proposed to Rose," Emery says as Rose sticks out her hand once more to show them the ring.

"Oh, what did she say?" his grandfather teases. "Did she say yes?"

Emery grins. "I think so."

Alice opens the windows in the library to air out the smoke. "This is absurd! We must leave until the smoke is gone. This is horrendous for our health. If you wish to die, so be it, but leave us out of it," she scolds her husband. "Come, children," she says to both Emery and Rose.

Meanwhile, Victoria is in her husband's office preparing the invitations for the engagement party. She is pleased to be throwing another social event, as she is quite the marvelous host. But this one will be the best of them all, right after Emery and Rose's wedding of course.

With Rose's permission, not one detail will be overlooked. Not if she is in charge.

❧◆❧

The Montgomery Estate is in chaos. As they receive their invitation formally by mail, a week later. Elizabeth Montgomery does her best to console her daughter.

Word travels quickly of Emery's engagement to a mysterious unknown American woman. But Elizabeth Montgomery takes it upon herself to investigate Rose. She hires a private detective to find out everything she can. Anything and everything she can use to her advantage.

"This isn't over, not just yet. He thinks we don't know," Elizabeth seethes to her daughter, bristling with anger as she sits at her dining room table.

"What else is there to do? He's marrying her," Juliet laments, sniffling through her tears. "It's over."

Mrs. Montgomery shakes her head. "Not by a long shot. This *nobody* is still married; do you know the scandal this will cause when I tell everyone?" she says to her daughter with a devilish grin. "He really thinks he can keep this from everyone? Ha!"

But poor Juliet only sobs into her hands. "This is my worst nightmare."

"We will play it cool; we have been invited to the engagement party. That is where I will confront him."

"And what do you think this will do for us?" Juliet challenges.

"Even if he won't marry you, the least I can do is sabotage his happiness with this nobody."

Mrs. Montgomery shakes her head in disgust.

"How could Victoria allow this? Her only son, the only heir

to the Williams' fortune, marrying this... American woman?" she sputters in disgust.

Juliet knows what her mother is plotting is horrible, but she won't stop her or foil her plans. Deep down, she too wishes to sabotage Emery's future with Rose. She can't help her jealous fury within.

"Make sure you look your best when we attend this engagement party," her mother tells her. "It is going to be quite the occasion."

Elizabeth Montgomery is set on her devilish plan.

"Oh, I don't think he will be marrying her. Not after this gets out."

As Victoria sends out the invitations to everyone, she has her hands full with endless things that need to be done. But she wouldn't have it any other way; she has been waiting for this day for quite some time.

"Can I help you with anything?" Rose asks Victoria.

"No, no. I've got it," she says adamantly. "You just relax, and I will do everything."

Emery calls up his good friend Theodore and invites him over to his parents' home. He wants him to meet Rose before the engagement party and to formally apologize for missing his wedding.

Theodore is delighted to hear from Emery. Before he can tell him the news of his engagement, Theodore himself tells him he had already heard. The news traveled quickly. He isn't one to gossip, but Emery's mystique and unpredictability keep people intrigued even more.

When he arrives at the house, Emery greets him with the warmest hug. Theodore arrives alone; his wife is on holiday with her parents. Theodore can't help himself; he grins from ear to ear at the sight of his friend.

"Well, well, well, it's finally happening for you," he says excitedly.

Rose sits in the living room with Alice, drinking tea. She can hear them both chatting as they stand in the foyer for a moment.

Emery beams with pure happiness. His piercing blue eyes are filled with so much light and hope for the future. "She is everything I wished for and more," he tells Theodore.

"I am glad to hear it. I wish you so much happiness. Truly."

Emery warmly embraces Theodore. "Come, you must meet her."

Theodore eagerly follows Emery into the living area where Rose sits by the fireplace. Upon their arrival, Rose glances up from her teacup to meet Theodore's gaze.

"Love, this is my good friend Theodore," Emery explains, introducing them.

She rises from her seat and holds out her hand to shake Theodore's. The ring on her finger immediately captures his attention.

"Oh my God!" Theodore blurts out, shaking Rose's hand. "That is… That's quite the statement piece," he says, stammering over his words.

Emery had forgotten for a moment about Theodore's search for the ring. Even more so, that the doctor who hired him to look for it is Rose's soon-to-be-ex-husband.

"It's an heirloom," Rose explains, offering a polite smile.

"I… I'm sorry, I just… can I see it?" Theodore asks, flustered.

Emery furrows his brow in concern.

"Sure," Rose says softly. She carefully takes the ring off her finger, and Emery watches his friend closely.

"I was searching for something that looks like this ring. Where on earth did you get this? Did you have it made?" Theodore asks Emery as he inspects it.

Emery moves closer to Rose.

"My grandfather gave it to me to give to Rose. It has been in my family for generations."

Theodore can hardly believe his eyes. "It is in amazing shape."

Emery nods. "If you must know, this is in fact the ring you were hired to look for," he explains. "I'm afraid your search has been in vain."

Theodore's eyes shoot up to look at him. "Are you serious?"

Alice glances at Theodore from where she sits across from Rose, confused. "You were hired to look for this ring?" she asks.

He clears his throat. "Yes," he answers reluctantly. "I was hired by someone to look for it; they wanted it for their wife."

Emery glances at Rose, becoming uncomfortable now aware of the connection between this ring, Emery, Rose, and Phillip.

"May I photograph it at least?" Theodore asks politely.

But Emery shakes his head. "I don't think that would be wise; the less people know about the existence of this ring the better."

Theodore tightens his lips and lowers his head.

"Who knows what kind of unwanted attention this could bring," Emery says.

Theodore nods. "I understand. Well, congratulations to you two! When's the wedding?"

"We have not set a date yet." Emery forces a smile.

Victoria walks in with a cold bottle of champagne in her hand. Nannie follows right behind her with flute glasses.

"Everyone! A toast is in order!" Victoria exclaims.

Chapter 19

R ose holds the champagne flute by the stem, observing as condensation forms on her glass, an uneasy feeling roiling in her gut.

Part of her feels as if things are moving too quickly. Yet Emery's face beams with happiness while gazing at Rose. He is obsessed with her and she with him, but the future seems so uncertain, even if they are getting married and are fully committing to one another.

What she had seen while under hypnosis with Victoria scares her; it rocks her sense of control. If Emery can't change his less than evolved behaviors, they won't make it, and just like Emery, Rose fears losing him.

Everyone is gathered in the living room, and Sir Ashby and Emery's grandfather opt for their usual drink of choice, brandy.

"Welcome to the family," Sir Ashby chimes to Rose as he begins his toast. "As you might have guessed, this family is far from perfect, just like every other family in this world. We do our best." He lets out a laugh as he says the last part.

Emery's grandfather nods in agreement.

"Unfortunately, however, we do come with some baggage of our own, which I am sure you are aware of by now. I want to assure you that we will protect you from the wolves that may come in sheep's clothing. It is not all smooth sailing in this family, and there will be ups and downs. But I promise you, we will do everything in our power to make sure you are —"

Rose shifts from one foot to the other and fidgets with her ring doing her best to ease her discomfort. Emery holds her close as his father speaks.

"As for me!" Victoria begins. Everyone laughs as she playfully cuts off Sir Ashby. "I am so happy that Emery has finally found his person. I know this is a dream come true for him and, who are we kidding? For us too. Maybe the ladies will settle down now."

Emery shakes his head slightly, embarrassed.

Theodore pats him on the back as he grins. "Oh, the horror! I can hear the hearts breaking now."

Emery's cheeks flush.

"Anyway!" Victoria continues laughing. "We are so happy for you two, and my sincerest hope is that you fall more in love with one another as time goes by. May you stick together through thick and thin. May the challenges that come bring you closer together. Be good to one another."

Everyone raises their glasses excitedly.

"Cheers!" Victoria says.

As they all sit around and chat, Theodore sits beside Rose on the sofa.

"Has he shown you the old abandoned estate nearby, where the woman who originally owned that ring lived?" he asks her inquisitively.

Rose looks at Theodore, intrigued. "He's mentioned it, but I haven't seen it."

Theodore raises his brows. "Well, I think he should take you to see it. It's cool."

Emery walks over from having a good chat with his grandfather to sit beside Rose.

"Why haven't you taken her to see the old estate we found the box at?" Theodore asks.

Emery's face perks up. "Haven't gotten around to it, but we will."

"There is a painting of the woman wearing that ring at the estate," Theodore tells Rose.

"Really?" she says captivated.

Theodore nods. "How is it that the ring came to be in your family again?" he asks Emery.

Unamused, Emery sighs. "It was my ancestors'."

"So, you're saying the woman in the painting at that old estate is related to you? How come there aren't any paintings of her in the gallery?"

"I don't know," Emery answers tightly.

"I know you lot have almost every member of the family in there."

"Yeah, I don't know."

"Maybe there's some sort of dark history there," Theodore presses.

Emery stares at his friend, growing annoyed. "Why won't you let this go?"

Theodore shrugs. "It's highly coveted by a lot of people. It's worth a lot. I'm just curious."

"I don't want to talk about it anymore," Emery snaps.

Theodore shrugs again, a bitter smile forms on his face. "Fine."

Rose sits there awkwardly, glancing between the two of them.

"Make sure you go see this place!" Theodore says to Rose. "It's interesting."

Rose nods. Emery walks away to get another glass. Victoria walks over and takes Emery's seat.

"How are you feeling?" she asks her.

By her demeanor, Rose can tell Victoria is having a great time. Slightly disheveled with a drink in hand, she starts going on about how the engagement party planning is coming along.

"You will be over the moon when you see the floral arrangements!" she begins. She covers her mouth as she laughs.

"What's so funny?" Theodore says, chuckling along.

"When she's drunk, everything is funny," Emery cuts in as he returns. "You took my seat," he quips at his mother.

"Yes, well… anyways. The floral arrangements are divine! They will cover all this area here," she says, waving her hand with a flourish. "It will look like an enchanted forest in here, you'll see. My grand vision will come to life!"

"I can't wait to see it," Rose chimes. "Thank you for everything."

Victoria pushes her hair out of her flushed face. "Oh, it's no problem. No problem at all."

Emery watches Theodore as he glances repeatedly at the ring on Rose's finger.

"Are you alright?" Emery asks him with raised brows, his hands resting on his hips. Shoulders tense.

Theodore shakes his head, he raises his hands in the air. "Are you sure I can't photograph it? I won't post it online or anything."

"No, man. I told you," Emery says assertively.

"Photograph what?" Victoria asks, cocking her head.

"The ring on Rose's finger," Theodore answers. "It is quite the myth of a piece!"

"Oh, I see," Victoria replies, glancing at the ring. "I'm afraid Emery is right, Theodore. I don't think that would be a good idea."

"It's so frustrating because it is such an exciting piece. It must be shared with the world," Theodore pleads.

Victoria shakes her head. "We don't need any more attention brought to us. Particularly with this ring. Do you have any idea the circus that would ensue? All the people wanting to buy it from us?"

"Mrs. Williams—"

"No, Theo," Victoria asserts. "I'm afraid the answer is no. See how persistent you are? Now, imagine the others that would come wanting it."

She shakes her head again at the mere thought.

"Just imagine, and you had even said so yourself, that an American man had hired you to search for it. He was willing to spend so much money to find it. Now that it is found, they wouldn't stop."

"Ever." Emery adds in almost a whisper.

Victoria nods.

"Fine. Can I at least come with you when you go to the old estate?" Theodore asks.

Emery nods. "Sure, if you promise to behave." He gives his friend a serious look.

"You have my word," Theodore swears, raising a hand in promise.

Victoria excuses herself for the night. But before she goes, she takes Rose with her.

"I need to talk to you," she whispers.

Rose follows Victoria upstairs.

"He was very persistent, wasn't he?" Victoria says to Rose quietly as they reach the top floor.

"I'd say so," Rose agrees, feeling uneasy about all the attention.

"Please, please be careful. Don't let him photograph your ring. Turn the emerald into your hand if you must when around Theodore."

"But what about at the party? People will eventually ask to see the ring even if they don't know about the history of it."

"Never mind that. No one is allowed to bring their phones in. The only photos being taken at the party will be from our camera men," Victoria assures her.

"Really?" Rose exclaims.

Victoria nods. "Oh, yes. Standard practice at my parties. People of status come here, and they want to be able to relax and let loose comfortably, knowing that no one is going to invade their privacy by recording them or taking photos without permission."

Chapter 20

Theodore and Emery arrange for a day to go visit the old estate. Rose is excited to see the place where Emery found the wooden box, as well. But when they arrive, Rose feels uncomfortable just looking at the place, further proving that everything they have seen is real.

"Isn't the old architecture great?" Theodore beams, looking out the window of their car.

"It is," Rose answers from the front seat, though she must force her voice not to waver.

"Do you think we would be able to take the painting with us?" Rose asks, turning to glance at Emery.

"The painting of the woman with the ring?" Emery asks for clarification. Pretending not to know what she means in front of his friend.

"I mean, I don't see why not? This place is abandoned," Theodore answers. "Why would you want it?"

"Well, the painting is part of the history of the ring," she argues.

Emery drives in carefully along what would have been the driveway.

Theodore gets out and opens Rose's car door for her.

"Let's go inside," he beckons, leading the way. Emery follows closely behind.

As Rose walks in, she takes a deep breath and looks around. It is incredibly eerie to her, as if she has walked into a time capsule.

Everything seems to be falling apart. The paint on the walls looks as if it has been scratched off with the passage of time. It appears that the home has sat abandoned without any attention since Emmett and Helena left the home back in the 18th century.

The furniture is still covered with linen cloths just as she had seen in her regressions. Everything is where it was left.

She walks up to the steps that lead to what was once Helena and Emmett's bedroom. The painting of Helena hangs on the wall, tattered and dusty.

"Holy shit!" Theodore blurts out.

Rose quickly turns to look at him, startled.

"You look just like her," he says, astounded. "Okay," he says, putting his hands together. "I don't know what is going on, but something... something is going on. And you need to tell me," Theodore says to Emery. "This is too weird."

Emery stays quiet as he glances over at Rose.

"You need to tell me," Theodore presses. "What is going on? The ring? Your family has it, and then she looks just like that woman. My instincts are going off."

Emery looks down at his feet. "You wouldn't believe me even if I told you."

"Try me," Theodore argues, waving a hand toward the rest of the house.

Emery grimaces. "God, I can't even bring myself to say it. I would sound insane."

Theodore stares at his friend, waiting for him to answer.

"No, I can't," Emery mutters. "I can't."

"I will figure it out, I promise you," Theodore retorts sharply. "I always do."

Emery simply shrugs. "Go for it, and let me know what conclusion you reach, besides it being an overwhelming coincidence."

Rose ignores them as she walks up the stairs and into the master bedroom. She can't help but wonder if Pierre's residence can be found. Emery walks in behind her.

"What are you thinking right now?" he whispers.

They stand there together in the room, a lofty silence building for a moment before she speaks.

"This is just more evidence, another incredible thing to add to the growing list."

"I'm going to see if I can get Theodore to help me take down the painting so we can bring it with us."

Emery walks off to find Theodore. Rose notices a vault in the closet and walks in to investigate, where she finds old letters and notes from Emmett to Helena. She takes all of them with her.

Back by the painting, Emery asks Theodore to help him remove the art piece from the wall, feeding his fascination further.

"Why do you want this painting so bad?" Theodore asks.

"Can you not?" Emery retorts.

"Why won't you tell me what is going on? First the box, the ring, and now this?" Theodore huffs.

Emery doesn't answer him and instead focuses on lowering the painting carefully to the floor.

"Are you on some sort of job I don't know about?" Theodore questions him further.

"No," he says simply. "I just don't know if I can tell you."

"Well, if you don't, then like I said, I will figure it out eventually," his friend snaps in response.

They finally get the painting down and load it into the car.

Rose walks outside to meet them and shows Emery the letters she found. Emery takes one from her and reads it before a smile spreads over his lips.

"This is a great find."

Rose grins in agreement. "Right?"

"Did you want to look around some more?" he asks.

"I don't know, maybe we can come just you and I another time?"

"Sure." Emery responds softly.

Theodore offers to drive back. Since he can't get much out of Emery, he tries his luck with Rose. "So, what are your thoughts about the fact that you look like this woman in the painting?" he asks her.

"I don't know what to think, but I do know that there are plenty of people on this planet who look alike." She shrugs.

Theodore raises a brow. "What do you plan to do with the painting?"

"I think most likely keep it as a sort of record or authentic relic. It's part of the ring's history and origin, so it's meaningful to have."

Theodore avoids eye contact and changes the subject, as he realizes he won't be getting anything out of Rose either.

"Should we go into town for some drinks? It's been a while," Theodore suggests.

Emery turns back to look at Rose, ignoring his suggestion.

"You can't hide forever," Theodore warns. "Eventually, the public is going to see you two. Might as well give them something. They will settle down after that."

"Or want to know more," Emery snips. "Once you open that door, it's hard to close it."

"So, what then? You plan to hide forever?"

"He's right," Rose says. "You can't."

"Is that a yes?" Theodore asks, glancing between the two of them.

Rose gives Emery the nod of approval.

"Let's go then," Emery tells his friend with a resigned sigh.

He selects a members' only club where they will have a better chance at some decent privacy. As they enter, some people's heads perk up at the sight of Emery, but they keep to themselves. The place is very beautiful; the velvet blue seating with gold finishes throughout make it glamorous yet inviting.

But the mirrors all around the room make it difficult for Rose to escape the gaze of other patrons. She attempts to avert her eyes.

"Here you go," Theodore says, handing Rose her drink.

"Thank you." She takes the glass in her hand but doesn't drink it.

Rose excuses herself to use the restroom. Emery watches as she leaves his side.

"Afraid she's going to run off?" Theodore quips.

Emery shrugs. "You never know."

"She might be realizing what she is getting herself into," Theodore says, only half teasing.

A concerned look comes over Emery's face. "I just don't want to lose her. I'm terrified that if I don't fuck this up, some outside force might."

Theodore sympathizes with him. "Honestly, I can't say your concerns aren't valid."

"Right?" Emery says with a grimace.

"Speaking of outside forces… how did Juliet take the news of your engagement?"

Emery sighs. "She's obviously not thrilled, I imagine. But I don't want to talk about that."

"Do you think her mother would try anything?"

"I wouldn't put anything past her mother," Emery whispers.

As the men chat at their table, a woman approaches Rose at the sink in the women's restroom. The woman stares at Rose and then at her ring finger as Rose places the ring back on.

"I'm sorry, are you Emery's fiancé?" the woman asks.

"Uh, yes," Rose answers quietly. "Do you know him?"

"Yes, I do."

The woman looks frazzled as she admires Rose.

"I didn't think he would come into town with you, since he is very private. Everyone is talking about his engagement, but no one has seen you. Do you know Elizabeth Montgomery?"

"I believe so. She is friends with Victoria Williams?" Rose says.

"Yes. That's right." The woman nods. "I've been invited to the engagement party, but I am happy to meet you now."

She extends her hand out to Rose.

"I'm Mary. Mary Pembleton," she says politely.

"I'm Rose."

"May I see the ring?" Mary asks eagerly with a smile. "I'm sorry, it's just… It's Emery Williams. I can't help but wonder what kind of ring he might choose."

Rose begins to feel a little uneasy by the woman's interest but shows her anyway. She extends her hand out to show her the emerald.

Mary's eyes sparkle at the sight of it. "Well, I wouldn't expect anything less," she chimes. "Marvelous!"

Rose smiles and excuses herself. "I must go now. Nice to meet you, Mary. I'll see you at the party then."

Mary watches Rose walk off in awe. Everyone is abuzz over Emery's engagement, and she is no exception.

Rose returns to the table.

"Do you know a Mary Pembleton?" she whispers to Emery.

"No," Emery answers with a pensive look.

"Well, a woman in the restroom stopped me and asked to see the ring. Apparently, she's been invited to the engagement party."

"Her name doesn't sound familiar. But around five hundred invitations have gone out," Emery admits. "She's most likely a family acquaintance."

"Oh," Rose says. "Well, her interest was a little off-putting."

Theodore grins. "Something you may want to get used to. The interest."

"That's becoming quite clear," she quips back.

Chapter 21

The morning of the engagement party, Rose lies beside Emery in bed and admires him as he sleeps.

Nannie knocks at the door to bring in their breakfast.

"Good morning," Rose says, opening the door.

"Morning," Nannie whispers back, handing over their food. "How are you feeling?"

"Nervous," Rose admits with a soft laugh.

"I would be lying if I said you shouldn't be," Nannie says quietly, trying not to wake Emery.

"Thanks," Rose retorts sarcastically.

Nannie smiles and makes her way out of the room. "Good luck!"

Rose closes the door and hops back into bed with Emery after setting down the food. She snuggles into his arms, enjoying the last few moments of peace that they will have for the day. She imagines they will most likely be pulled in a million directions with everyone wanting to spend time with them at the party.

"Wake up," Rose whispers in his ear, craving more than just sleeping in bed.

She kisses him awake. His blue eyes open at her drowsily.

"That's one way to wake up," Emery mutters.

He tries to go back to sleep, but Rose isn't having it. Knowing one of his weaknesses, she kisses his neck slowly, enticing him to make his move.

After a few tantalizing kisses, Emery is wide awake, and he assertively and dominantly places her body underneath his. His lips devour her body ardently kiss by kiss. As his penis hardens, he pushes her panties to the side and gently slides into Rose.

Her lips meet his passionately, and Emery peers into Rose's eyes, conveying what words could never say. So, he shows her instead, allowing his body and soul to do the talking. While he thrusts deeper and deeper into Rose, he puts his hand over her mouth to avoid anyone hearing them.

She can't help herself; the pleasure is formidable. Drunk off the devilish pleasure he gives her, Rose closes her eyes and moans.

"Open your eyes," Emery whispers.

She does as he says. Her gaze meets his in an ardent dance of deep love and desire, and they climax together. Paralyzed with pleasure, she holds Emery inside a little while longer.

He doesn't fight her and rests his body on hers.

"I love you," Rose says to Emery, savoring this moment.

"Je t'aime," Emery whispers back, his expression flushed.

"Time to get ready." She smirks.

She gets up to turn on the shower, and her silk nightgown falls to the floor as she enters, closing the door behind her. The water falls from the showerhead onto her face as she closes her eyes.

Moments later, the shower door opens again, and the water is interrupted from falling on her. Emery's lips feverishly press onto hers while her eyes are still closed, igniting her passion for him once more.

His tongue forcefully finds its way into her mouth as his hands grasp her body closer to his. Rose finds herself enslaved to his every desire.

She pushes her bottom back on Emery while he enters her again, this time not as gentle as usual, but it is exactly what she craves. This time, they can be as loud as they want; the shower muffles out any noise.

Emery presses her against the shower wall and allows his passion for Rose to have free reign. Both allow their insatiable lust for one another to take over. Emery's hands enmesh themselves in Rose's hair, pulling at it unhesitatingly. Rose doesn't stand a chance at lasting very long and explosively orgasms. Emery grips her hips to keep her in place as he finishes soon after.

Breathlessly, she rests her head on his chest to catch her breath while they stand under the water together. Holding one another, in that exact moment, both know without a shadow of a doubt that they are simply always meant to be.

Rose stands in Emery's embrace as her eyes fill with tears. The surge of emotions rises in her chest; no one has ever made her feel the way he does. She feels it in her heart center, and her rational mind still cannot comprehend any of it.

"Why are you crying?" Emery asks softly.

"I don't know," she answers. "I honestly don't know."

His mesmerizing gaze investigates hers, concerned. He holds her tighter in his arms as fear rises within him.

"I want to say I love you, but I feel like those words just don't suffice," Emery tells her.

"Then find new words," Rose whispers.

He thinks for a moment as he holds her.

"When you breathe, so do I. When you hurt, I hurt," he says earnestly. Emery's hands move to graze Rose's face, as they gently guide her gaze to his. The tears in his eyes give way to Rose's. "When you look, I look too. Our hearts beat as one, and know that if your heart ever stops beating, so does mine."

His poetic words linger in her psyche and imprint themselves onto her soul as they hold one another a little while longer.

◦◦◈◦◦

Guests begin to trickle into the Williams' estate, in amazement of Victoria's decorations for the engagement party. In the bedroom, Emery puts on his tailored suit as Rose gets dressed. He can tell she is lagging.

"Are you nervous?" he asks with a soft smile.

They can both now hear the commotion of the guest's downstairs.

"Over five hundred people have been invited," Rose says as her voice shakes. "That's a lot for anyone."

He nods. "I know." He comes to sit beside Rose on the bed. "We don't have to do this, you know."

Rose shakes her head. Emery takes her hand in his for support.

"I just wonder if we should slow down," she admits.

Rose's hand trembles while she wipes a cold sweat off her forehead.

"Are you getting cold feet?" Emery asks, placing his hand over his heart.

Rose walks off into the restroom. She stands there looking at herself in the mirror, frozen in place.

Don't self-sabotage, a wiser voice within her says.

Emery stands at the door, his hand extended out to hers. "We will do this together," he assures her.

Rose nods and takes his hand. They walk to the door together; as Emery opens the door, the roar of the party downstairs is lively. From the top of the steps, Rose can see the inside of the home has been transformed into an enchanted forest. It takes Rose's breath away immediately.

The walkways are lined with moss and hydrangeas. The ceiling of the home appears as the night sky. The twinkling effect of the lights adds a mystical tone.

Rose peers down at the crowd of people below, biting her lip.

"Holy shit," she whispers.

Emery squeezes her hand. "Ready?"

Rose takes a deep breath and nods. Emery is nervous too, but he's had years to get used to these sorts of things, while Rose is accustomed to a quiet and peaceful life without much attention.

She struggles to stop herself from self-sabotaging and running away as fast as she can.

But she knows she would be an absolute fool to walk away from this love.

As Emery and Rose walk down the steps together, people start to take notice of them and gleefully greet them. Victoria quickly makes her way over from where she was mingling.

"Oh, good! You're ready," she says to them. "You both look so good together."

From where Emery stands, he spots Juliet and the rest of the girls he grew up with. He looks at Juliet stoically. Her eyes glare at Rose with bitter envy, but she keeps her distance.

Despite their grievances, Elizabeth and Juliet were not uninvited by his mother Victoria. His mother, unlike Elizabeth Montgomery, is a very refined and tolerant woman, and she figured Mr. Montgomery, Sir Ashby's good friend, should not have to bear any punishment for his wife's or daughter's misdeeds and miss out on this joyous moment.

As Emery watches Juliet, he pulls Rose closer to him.

Everyone is eager to meet Rose and talk to her, but he won't let her out of his sight.

Victoria bounces around the entire party, joyously having the time of her life. Sir Ashby and his parents are seated at their table, talking to the many people that pass by. Emery guides Rose over as they greet people on the way.

"I'm afraid you won't be able to sit down much," Sir Ashby says to his son, laughing. "How are you holding up?" he asks Rose, aware she must be overwhelmed.

"Frazzled," Rose answers, forcing a smile.

Victoria orchestrates a waltz that everyone can join in on, placing Emery and Rose at the center.

"I don't know how to dance," Rose whispers to Emery, her eyes widened in panic.

"We will improvise!" he says fearlessly.

All eyes are on them, and she can feel it as people shamelessly stare her down.

"Don't falter on me," Emery whispers in her ear.

"I'm trying not to."

Emery struggles to keep her attention. "Just look at me. Focus on me."

And it works for a little while; the party and setup of things seem like a blast from their past. She can only wonder if Victoria did it on purpose. Emmett and Helena danced a waltz just like this one in their time.

While Rose looks into Emery's eyes, she can't help but smile. He centers her in a way no one can. As Rose focuses her attention on Emery throughout the night, she can't help but feel some women's judgmental gazes on her.

She notices a familiar face sitting beside Juliet and Elizabeth Montgomery. It is Mary, the woman she had met at the pub in London.

From what she can tell, it appears that they are talking about her as Mrs. Montgomery whispers something to Mary. But they are not the only ones; other women at their tables and throughout the party are also behaving in the same manner.

Rose can only chalk it up to petty envy or something of the sort. After the waltz, Victoria announces a surprise she has planned for Emery and Rose outside in the garden and lawn area. Everyone makes their way outside, eager to see what awaits them. It is cold, and the night sky is clear.

Theodore and his wife make their way towards Emery and Rose.

"Hello!" Emery gushes excitedly. "You're here!"

Theodore gives Emery a tight hug.

"I was trying to work my way to you, man! These people don't make it easy!" Theodore admits.

The whole night has been quite the blur. Rose can hardly keep track of faces and names that she has met throughout the evening.

"How are you?" Theodore asks Rose as he gives her a hug next.

"Okay." She responds before tightening her lips and widening her eyes.

"Overwhelmed?" Theodore says through laughter.

"Something like that." She shrugs.

"Hi, I'm Samantha," Theodore's wife says, introducing herself to Rose.

"Ah, yes. This is my wife. Wife, meet Rose. Rose, meet wife," Theodore says playfully.

"Nice to meet you," Rose tells Samantha with a smile.

Victoria gives the signal, and the first firework goes off. Like a shooting star flying across the night sky, the firework illuminates the clouds above them. Emery holds Rose close and places his jacket on her. Victoria has truly outdone herself with the party. It is a night to remember.

After a little while, Rose and Emery take a walk alone through the rose garden as the fireworks continue to light the night sky. But soon, their moment of bliss is interrupted by Elizabeth Montgomery.

She glares at Rose from head to toe in disgust.

"Now I understand why you didn't want to marry Juliet," she says angrily to Emery.

"Excuse me?" Emery rounds on her.

"You apparently like them married," she slyly says.

Emery moves to stand in front of Rose protectively. "What did you just say?"

"You heard me," Mrs. Montgomery retorts. "She's a married woman, engaged to you. The scandal this is!" She scoffs.

Victoria overhears them from where she stands and walks over briskly. "What is going on over here?" she asks Mrs. Montgomery.

Juliet soon walks up behind her mother.

"He's engaged to a married woman. Did you think no one would know?" Juliet says to Victoria.

Victoria's body tenses, while she pivots her fiery gaze to Juliet. "She's separated," Victoria corrects her.

"She's married," Mrs. Montgomery says again.

Rose holds onto Emery's arms as she stands behind him. The shame and embarrassment consume her as she realizes that everyone in the party must know. Mrs. Montgomery took it upon herself to inform everyone what she had discovered about Rose.

The party guests have now overheard them too. Curious, they look over to see what the fuss is about. Everyone is now staring at them instead of watching the fireworks that are going off. It is clear this is an ambush orchestrated by Juliet and her mother to tear Emery and Rose apart.

"You would stoop so low," Victoria seethes, getting in Mrs. Montgomery's face.

"I would stoop so low? Look at you! Covering up for your son's indiscretion!" she yells back.

Victoria slaps her as hard as she can.

The party guests erupt in gasps and whispers. What a scandal, indeed.

Chapter 22

"Victoria," Juliet tries. She takes a step back shaking.

"Get out of my house!" Victoria shouts. "You have crossed a line there is no coming back from!"

Emery has never seen his mother this angry. In fact, no one ever has, not even Sir Ashby.

"Get out!" she shouts once more, her face turning red. "I never want to see you again. Get out!"

Victoria's estate security swiftly arrives to escort Juliet and her mother out of there.

Emery hugs Rose, but in that moment, she wishes to be anywhere but here. From Emery's embrace, she watches as the party guests gawk at her from where they stand, and she understands now why everyone was looking at her the way they were throughout the evening. All judging her and gossiping about her without her knowing, thanks to Mrs. Montgomery.

Jack Montgomery, Elizabeth Montgomery's husband, tries to apologize profusely to no avail.

"Please, Jack, leave," Sir Ashby tells his friend, heavy-hearted. "Please go."

Rose doesn't quite know what to do with herself. All she knows is that she needs to get out of here immediately. She makes her way inside the house and runs up to Emery's room. She is completely humiliated.

Rose begins to abruptly pack all her belongings. Emery opens the bedroom door to see her stuffing her things into her bag and begins to panic.

"Don't do this!" he says frantically. "Please stop."

But Rose continues to pack everything up. "I'm leaving. I feel sick to my stomach. I shouldn't have come here."

Emery closes Rose's suitcase and tries to put it in the closet. "You're not leaving me."

Rose begins to sob on the bed from embarrassment. "Everyone knew... everyone," she says, replaying the evening in her head.

Emery sits beside her, struggling to calm her. "This is what they want. They want to tear us apart. Don't give it to them. Please."

Rose shakes her head. "I want to go home."

Emery watches the tears fall from Rose's eyes, his chest tightens, and his heart feels as if a dagger is being driven right through it.

All the guests leave. It is now after 3 a.m. Per Rose's request, Ferdi loads up her bags into the car. Sir Ashby and Victoria lend Rose the family plane to return to her home as she wishes, and she will be departing soon.

Before leaving, Rose stands outside for a moment by the pond watching as the starlight reflects off the water. She wipes a tear from the corner of her eye. Emery walks up behind her, and she stiffens.

"Please don't leave me," he says, pleading as if his life depends on it. "Why are you running instead of fighting for us?"

Rose reluctantly answers, "We never stood a chance, Emery. It's time to wake up to the truth."

The disbelief in Emery's gaze is prevalent.

"Wishful thinking will get us nowhere," Rose cynically

continues. "Meant to be or not, there is just so much uncertainty."

"You're saying our love is just wishful thinking? What about everything we feel for one another? Are you saying that what we have experienced isn't real?"

"That's exactly what I'm saying," Rose mutters.

In disbelief, Emery's eyes fill with tears.

"It won't work, Emery. It didn't before; why would it now?"

Rose tries to walk away from him, but he grabs her hand before she can get away.

"Because it's meant to be. In every lifetime, don't you see? It's you and me." He pauses. His eyes peer into Rose's as they reflect heartbreak. A single tear falls from them. "I would never give up hope that we would work."

Rose pulls away from him. "Well, aren't you a fool?"

Emery's lips form a desolate smile. "For you, yes." The pain in his tone is evident. "A hopeless fool. You are the great love of my infinite existence."

Emery pulls her close to him, and he rests his forehead on hers.

"Stay with me," he begs. "Please stay with me."

Rose can't bring herself to stay, no matter how much Emery pleads. She needs to be alone for a while. "I need to go home," she answers. "Please respect that."

Emery brings his hands to his head, his hopeless eyes transfixed on her. An audible short and sharp breath escapes his mouth. "I can't lose you. I won't," he says adamantly. "Is this it? Is this the end?" His tone becomes increasingly frantic. "Call me a fool all you want; I'd rather be a fool than a coward!" Emery shouts angrily.

He can't contain his frustration. The love they share is

beyond understanding, so passionate and consuming. He can't understand how she could so easily walk away from it. He takes her hand in his and places it over his heart.

"I love you, madly, infinitely and without any reservations... you are the one for me. I know this with absolute certainty," he pleads.

Rose stares at him; the devastation on his face is too much for her to take. Her eyes well up and her view of him becomes blurred through her tears.

"You're the love of my life. I need you to know that" she says, trying to pull her hand away.

Emery hangs on every word as if it were his oxygen, refusing to let her go. "Please don't do this."

He pulls her into his arms. Her lips melt into his; it is hard to define what he does to her. Emery's hands grip her body's curves. She struggles to understand the push and pull between them.

"I have to go..." Rose whispers. She kisses him again before walking away from Emery to the waiting car. He trails behind her like a lost puppy.

Rose reluctantly leaves him in the driveway, pleading. Ferdi begins to drive away with Rose. Victoria stands behind Emery quietly. Observing him as he watches Rose leave; Emery falls to his knees.

Victoria knows that Rose isn't leaving simply because she was embarrassed by the Montgomerys at the party. This energy of hesitation has been building within her for some time now, ever since she had undergone her progression with the assistance of Victoria.

The choice was never meant to be easy; she too is being tested. But will she make the right choice?

"Let her go," she says softly.

Emery turns to look at his mother with anguish.

"I know. But you must let her go."

Emery hardly sleeps or eats for weeks to come. Rose returns to Carmel by-the-sea alone. She doesn't talk to Emery for weeks; the space allows her to clear her mind and take space for herself.

Rose meditates and sits in her home alone on some days and others she can't help but overthink everything that has happened. Her evenings are spent sitting on the front porch wrapped in a warm blanket peering vacantly at the ocean across the street. The grey skies match her sentiments.

On one evening much to her surprise, Phillip pays her a visit.

Rose opens the door but keeps her gaze down at his feet.

"Hi," he says warmly. "You're back."

Phillip observes Rose and can't help but notice that she appears downcast, making very little eye contact she isn't quite herself.

"May I come in?" Phillip asks.

Rose shrugs. "Sure."

They sit down across from one another in the living room.

"How have you been?" Phillip asks.

"A lot has happened," she answers. "Would you like something to drink?"

"Just water is fine." He looks at Rose uneasily. Afraid Emery may show up any minute.

She brings him a cup of water and sits back down across from him on the sofa in the living room. "How are you? Still busy with work?" Rose asks him to make small talk. She sips her ginger tea, awaiting his answer.

"I've actually taken some time off."

Rose raises her brows. "That's interesting."

Phillip stares at her longingly. "I… I want you back."

Rose glances briefly back at Phillip, she wraps her blanket around her body. Her gaze fixed on anything but him. "Please—"

"I know this is stupid; maybe *I'm* stupid. I didn't work hard enough for us. I just let you go too easily."

"Phillip…" she trails off, at a loss for words.

"I am here to ask for another chance. We can start over—"

"I'm pregnant," Rose blurts out, interrupting him.

Her words cut through him like a knife.

"What—"

Phillip struggles to say.

"I just found out a day ago," she whispers.

He sighs, throwing his hands in the air "Of course, you are. That fucking bastard!" Phillip angrily shouts.

"I can't deal with this right now. Please calm down," Rose says, her voice shakes without strength.

"No, he fucking did this on purpose! I just know it. I just fucking know it!" Phillip's voice grows louder it resounds off the walls in the home. Pacing back and forth, his hands tightened into fists. "So, I guess that's it then; he's won. He can't win you fairly, so he stoops so low to keep you this way. By getting you pregnant."

Rose frowns at Phillip. "He doesn't even know, Phillip. I haven't told him."

He shakes his head. "You give him the benefit of the doubt too much, you know that? He isn't as honorable as you think," he snaps, losing his patience. "He's deceitful and underhanded. You refuse to see it; he wants you at any cost. Even if it isn't in your best interest. How could that possibly be love?"

"Oh, and like you know anything about love. You prioritized your work over me. You of all people shouldn't be talking. You don't have a leg to stand on."

"I fucked up. I know that. But you're blinded. You're not seeing things clearly."

"You don't even know him!" Rose argues. She gets up from where she sits to open her front door. "Please leave. I need to rest."

Devastated, Phillip observes her from where he sits.

"You know I'd still want to be with you, despite it all," he says, confessing. "I still love you."

Rose grips her blanket tighter around her body and steps back from him. In fact, she refuses to look at Phillip. "I am not having this conversation with you."

"Why not?" Phillip presses. "I want you despite everything. If you choose me, we can be a family again."

Rose stares at him in disbelief. "I know you did not just say that to me."

But Phillip means every word. "It kills me to know that you're with him. But it's not over for me. You're still my wife."

"You let our marriage go to shit and you come in here and think you can just have me back? You're fucking joking, right? You prioritized work over me, and now because Emery is in my life, you want me back?"

"I have never stopped loving you. I work a lot, I know, and I can change that. If you choose me, I will be home more. I promise."

"You need to leave," Rose mutters. "Now."

Phillip feels he's lost her forever. The news has delivered a crushing blow to his hopes of reconciling. Defeated for the time being, he makes his way out of the home they once shared together. He too is true to his sentiments of love for Rose. *His heart will never let her go.*

Even if he is forced to move on physically, his heart will always want her, even if she doesn't want him in return.

144

Chapter 23

Back in England, Emery confides in his mother about his heartache. He feels as if his heart has been ripped out of his chest.

"I can't be without her," Emery says to his mother through tears. "I know how stupid I sound, but I will die without her."

Victoria watches as the tears drip down his cheeks. "Just take a deep breath. Things will calm down soon; are you following her back to Carmel?" she asks tenderly.

Emery shakes his head. "I don't know. She said she needed space."

"I think you should go to her," Victoria tells him.

Rose drives to see Catherine without an appointment. She just couldn't wait; she needs someone to talk to who understands. In a hurry, Rose walks up the steps to Catherine's front door and knocks loudly.

It's begun to rain heavily, and she knows she shouldn't be here, but she needs to see her, Rose needs her guidance.

Catherine finally opens the door, alarmed by the sudden knocking. She is pleasantly surprised to see Rose but is puzzled as to why she's visiting. By the look on her face, however, she assumes it must be urgent.

"Rose," Catherine says in surprise.

"I'm sorry, I just really needed to talk to you."

Catherine moves aside to let her inside. "Come in. How are things?" she asks Rose. "How is Emery?"

Rose stays quiet for a moment; she takes a seat on the couch and appears paralyzed with fear. "I'm pregnant," she blurts out.

Catherine sits beside her. "Oh, I see," she murmurs. By the look on Rose's face, she isn't sure if she should congratulate her or not. "How are you feeling about it?"

Rose looks down at her hands. "I love Emery. I really do, but the uncertainty of the future is hard to deal with. I saw something while under hypnosis by his mother, and..." she pauses. "I am afraid it may come true."

Catherine rests her hand on hers, trying to comfort her. "The future is fluid. Nothing is ever set in stone." She offers a reassuring smile.

"I don't know, this felt real, almost like a warning. If we don't get it right, the worst could happen," Rose says, wiping a tear away.

"I think this is a moment in your life when you really need to trust your intuition."

Rose shakes her head and rises from where she sits; she begins to anxiously pace back and forth. "That's the thing. I don't know what to trust. I love him, and I want to be with him. I know we are meant to be together, but it isn't easy. I have so many fears."

"Don't give in to them," Catherine says, and she slightly raises her right brow. "Although, there is no going back now, you're expecting his child. I imagine you've made your choice?"

Rose looks down at her hand; her ring finger is bare.

"Yes, I have," she answers with a tremble in her voice. "I know we belong to each other. But these fears... I almost feel as if I would be better off alone and not choosing either Phillip or Emery. As if by not choosing either I can protect myself?"

Catherine shakes her head. "That is your ego talking. Protect yourself from what? The greatest love of your life?"

Rose begins to cry. "It's the fear of losing it. Of allowing myself to really love him wholeheartedly. If I lose him at the end of it all, I am the one left with all the pain."

She looks at Catherine, distraught.

"I could never survive that... losing Emery."

Catherine walks over to hug her. "Choose love. Choose optimism. By giving into the fear, you breathe life into it." She gives her a serious look.

Catherine's words struggle to make an impact on Rose. Her fear is far too great.

"Where is Emery now?" she asks.

"Back home."

Catherine nods. "Don't be your own worst enemy. You're trying to talk yourself out of the greatest love of your life."

Rose breaks down in Catherine's arms further.

"Does Emery know you're pregnant?"

Rose shakes her head.

"Tell him," Catherine instructs her.

They spend time talking, as it helps calm Rose. She tells Catherine about everything that happened while in England. All the stuff they've found, the island they visited, and Helena and Emmett's grave site, as well as the humiliating moment with Mrs. Montgomery and her daughter.

As Rose relays to Catherine how everything occurred, she can't help but feel incredibly angry and perplexed at the lengths that some people are willing to go out of jealousy and sheer refusal to accept someone's rejection.

"I was completely embarrassed," Rose states, shaking her

head in disbelief. "The gall of some people. That woman should be embarrassed."

Catherine feels bad for Rose, and she observes the mortified expression on her face. "Yes, that is terrible. I'm sorry you had to go through that." She squeezes Rose's hand in support. "How did Emery handle the ordeal? He must've been very upset."

"He stood in front of me and was very protective. He did his best to shut it down, but it was futile. Everyone at the party was watching."

Rose looks away, remembering the moment and becoming embarrassed as if it were happening again.

"It was awful. I left as soon as I could. I couldn't stay there any longer. His family has been lovely to me, but his social world is very different from mine."

Catherine shrugs. "Are you going to let that deter you from being with him?" she asks softly. Her green eyes admire Rose, awaiting a response. "If you do, you will be giving those women what they want."

Rose looks at her solemnly.

"If you want real, true love, you must be willing to fight for it. No matter how meant to be you are, both of you need to put in effort to protect your relationship from outside influences," Catherine continues. "From what I gather, Emery seems more than willing to fight for you and the relationship, But I fear you are letting the fear of the unknown eat you up alive."

"It's pain I fear," Rose answers with a sniffle.

Catherine smiles tightly. "It's a part of life, is it not?" she reminds her.

"It is, I just can't find the strength to overcome the fear."

Catherine squeezes Rose's hand a little more before releasing it. "I am confident you will find it."

Rose knows she needs to speak with Emery as soon as

possible. She wonders if she should call him and tell him about the news over the phone but fears it may be too impersonal. Suddenly, there is a knock at the door. Catherine rises from her seat and opens it.

"Hi!" says a cheerful woman. "Oh, I'm so sorry, did I interrupt?" she adds quickly, seeing Rose sitting on the couch.

"No, no," Catherine replies with a big smile.

Rose gets up from where she sits and walks over to the door, not wanting to keep the woman from her appointment with Catherine.

"I'll talk to you later," she says to Catherine as she lets herself out. "Excuse me," Rose says kindly to the woman.

"Take care of yourself." Catherine calls out to Rose on her way out.

Chapter 24

Emery arrives in Carmel with a great sense of urgency. He was going to reach out to Rose and let her know he was heading back to her, but he feared she might have asked him to stay away longer than he could bare.

After being dropped off at his local home, Emery walks over to Rose's house.

He begins to get nervous as he approaches her door. Finally, he works up the courage to knock and waits for a few seconds before the door opens. From the look on Rose's face, it is obvious she is completely shocked to see him at her doorstep.

Seeing her face to Emery feels as if he has collected a fresh breath in his lungs. "Hi," he greets her nervously.

Rose struggles for words.

"May I come in?" he asks. His soulful blue eyes peer at her, meekly.

Rose nods but is still quite in shock. Once inside, they sit down together by the window in the little breakfast nook.

"I didn't know you were in town," Rose begins softly.

"I just got here; I came straight here." He shrugs.

Rose looks out the window to the ocean.

"I couldn't be away from you anymore. I know you said you needed space... and I'm sorry for barging in on you like this. But I had to see you."

"After what happened, I was completely embarrassed," Rose confesses. "I needed this time."

Emery takes her hand in his.

"I have something to tell you," Rose says as she turns to look at him.

His eyes watch her nervously, fearing she may have had a change of heart and might want to call off their engagement.

Rose gets up from where she sits and walks over to her kitchen drawer where she pulls out a piece of paper and brings it over to Emery.

"I am pregnant," she tells him. A soft smile forms on her face. "I was feeling off when I got back and thought maybe it was just the jet lag, but after not getting my period, I went to my doctor and found out there."

Emery's face lights up like the sun. He smiles from ear to ear, overjoyed. He reads the document from Rose's doctor, confirming her pregnancy.

"This is incredible!" he exclaims. "How do you feel? Have you been getting plenty of rest?"

Rose sits down beside him. "Yes, I have been trying. My body does feel different, and I feel a bit off. But I suppose that's normal."

The conversation feels superficial and awkward. It is hard to address what happened back at their engagement party. But the conversation needs to be had.

"I am beyond happy. If I was to have children with anyone, you are that person," Emery says to her, helplessly in love. "I don't know how to address what happened back home. I'm sorry for everything. I tried to protect you; I really did. This is why I was so happy to be as private and *under the radar* as possible. I feared they may try to sabotage our connection."

"How did they know anything about me?" Rose questions him, frowning slightly.

Emery shakes his head. "They must've investigated you. Private detectives of some sort." Rose shakes her head angrily. He continues, "I am incredibly angry at how they violated your privacy. Unfortunately, I feared it would be something that could possibly happen."

Rose rolls her eyes, unamused. "I don't want to talk about this anymore," she mutters.

"Is this everything you wanted to hash out?"

"I think so." Rose answers. She closes her soft cardigan and wraps it around her body. "Our lives are going to change forever, you know that. This baby changes everything."

Emery nods. His eyes still fixated on her. "I know," he answers. "I am prepared for that."

They sit closely next to each other, hand in hand.

"Where do we go from here?" Emery asks. "I love you; you know that" he says softly. "I meant what I said when I called you the great love of my infinite existence... you are."

Rose peers at him as a soft smile forms across her face. He can pull her towards him without even trying. His essence is alluring and lovely.

It is time she accepts that they will always come back to each other; their love is far from perfect, but it is true. They challenge one another and shine a light on each other's shadows, forcing them to heal.

"I love you, too," Rose begins. "I have been so cynical and blind. I called you a fool and thought of you as a fool because you allowed yourself to believe in love. In us."

She looks down at her feet as her eyes form tears.

"The truth is, I have been the biggest fool of all."

Rose turns her gaze to Emery as he listens.

"I am not the most emotionally expressive person, I know this. But I have been so afraid to allow myself to fully love you out of fear of losing you. But it has been futile." Rose wipes a tear away. "I have been a fool to think that I could only half love you. What I feel for you consumes me if I allow myself to feel it all…"

"Feel it all," Emery encourages her. He leans his face closer to hers. "You can't do anything in half measures. Especially in love."

Rose nods. "I am scared to."

"Living that way is no way to live at all, Rose."

Despite what fate has in store for them, Rose is certain their love can overcome any challenges that might appear. She looks into Emery's eyes and kisses his lips passionately. This man is the love of her life, the man she chooses to be with.

"Let yourself go," Emery whispers breathlessly. "I will not allow you to love me halfway."

Her hands grip his neck while she kisses him some more. Emery's hands grip her body firmly, the passion between them simmering.

"Let's go upstairs," Rose says, growing aroused.

Without hesitation, Emery follows her lead. Unable to wait to get to the bedroom, Emery takes Rose on the stairs.

He presses his groin into her backside, and she can feel his erection through their clothes. Her hand slips down to his zipper to help relieve his erect penis out of his pants. Emery takes control of Rose's hips by placing his hands on each side.

Kneeling on the stairs, Rose stays put, and Emery pulls her silk dress up. His soft hands push her panties to the side. His penis slowly enters her, eliciting a soft moan from Rose's lips.

Emery builds momentum with each thrust he gives her. Her breathless moans fill the stairwell, and Rose twists around just enough to meet Emery's lips, arousing her further and pushing her to orgasm powerfully.

His arms now wrap around her body, holding it against his own. Emery delicately sinks his teeth into Rose's neck as he finishes inside of her.

Her hands grip his as she comes down from the enthralling high. They laugh together, delightfully pleased by one another. Rose sits on the steps while Emery rests beside her. Dainty drops of sweat glisten on his forehead, his hair sexily disheveled.

Rose playfully grips his hair in her hand and tugs at it. "I think my knees are going to bruise," she says, looking down at her legs.

Emery smirks. "Maybe."

He scoops Rose up in his arms and carries her to the bedroom. They rest on the bed beside one another. Emery caresses Rose's womb area, admiring it for a moment.

"I'm going to be a dad," he says as the news sinks in further.

"Are you nervous?" Rose asks softly.

Emery peers at her. "No. I am excited." He shuffles closer. "I love you," he whispers. "I love you with all that I am. Every breath I breathe is yours."

Rose moves to rest on his chest. "Every beat of my heart is yours," she replies.

Emery grips her body; his lips kiss her head as it rests on his chest.

"We are going to be parents," he says to her. "Parents!" The joy in his voice is contagious. "I am unbelievably happy."

Rose smiles at him, her eyes becoming heavy-lidded as she begins to let herself fall asleep on him.

Emery snuggles Rose in his arms, eventually falling asleep himself.

Chapter 25

Rose wakes up just before dawn to see Emery is not beside her in bed.

She gets up to change into her silk nightgown and throws a long coat over it. She tiptoes down the stairs to the living room and spots Emery in front of the fireplace. The fire is going, warming up her cottage home nicely.

"What are you doing up?" Rose asks, peering at the flickering flames.

"Hmm?" Emery says raising his brows as he glances over his shoulder at her.

"You're up so early." She shrugs.

"Oh, yes. I feel well-rested," Emery says. "I'm sorry if I woke you."

"No, no," Rose says, snuggling up next to him. "The fire feels nice."

Her eyes heavy lidded struggle to remain open.

"Do you want me to hold you until you fall asleep?" he whispers in her ear.

Rose nods. Emery takes her in his arms and embraces her, and Rose buries her face in his neck, cuddling into him. His arms are her home now; there is nowhere else she'd rather be.

Rose loves him madly, deeply, and fearlessly. He sets her

soul on fire; moving past her fears, she can finally allow herself to be happy.

The moment she takes this step, unbeknownst to her, she passes her portion of the lesson.

By choosing Emery once and for all, she chooses love over fear.

Although she loved Phillip dearly, her heart was holding onto him out of fear. Part of the lesson of love is learning to let go, letting go of the people we love when the relationship has run its course and surrendering to what fate has designed.

Emery is Rose's highest path; Phillip served his purpose in teaching her that not all relationships are meant to last a lifetime and that when the time comes, we must release them with love.

As Emery holds Rose, he can't help but envision everything he has planned for their future. He hopes that he can stay in Carmel and raise his child there with Rose instead of England. But he also knows the pressure from his father is going to mount as soon as he tells Sir Ashby that Rose is pregnant. His father will expect Emery to raise his family back home and not in the States.

If he had been honest with Rose, he would have confessed that as the reason he woke up earlier than he wanted to. His father is relentless and will not give up so easily.

While enjoying the warmth from the fireplace, Emery notices the sun rising as the early sunlight begins to spill in through the front windows, bathing the room in a warm glow.

Rose grips Emery's hand as she slips in and out of sleep. Emery lifts her hand up to his lips, playfully nibbling on her skin to wake her. She fidgets but stays asleep, a sight which makes him smile.

Resigned to allow her to rest, he decides to get up from where he lies to make some coffee. He carefully places Rose on the sofa, before walking over to the kitchen barefoot, he wishes he'd grabbed some clothes from his place.

He opts for one of Rose's throw blankets off the couch and wraps it around himself to fight off the morning chill. The espresso machine is excessively loud, so he peeks over at Rose, afraid it might have woken her up.

Biting his lip, he continues when he sees she sleeps through the noise. As he makes his latte, Emery becomes lost in pensive thought. He remembers his past life in the eighteenth century, his mistakes, and emotional pain. It still lingers in his present moment; intrusive thoughts enter his mind that he will never completely have Rose.

He understands why she holds back—he truly does. But he will not let fear stop him from experiencing her. He knows without a shadow of a doubt that he has never in all his existence loved someone the way he intoxicatingly loves her.

With a contented sigh, Emery makes his way to the little balcony in front of the home that looks out over at the beach in the distance, latte in hand. The soft frothed milk atop his coffee lines his lips as he takes a sip.

A woman with her little terrier dog and sun hat walks past. She waves at him from across the street. He waves back as he wraps his blanket around himself a little tighter. The breeze is cool against his face. Emery can hear the waves crashing on the shore beyond the road, symphony to his ears.

Truly, he can't imagine raising his child anywhere else. The scenery is peaceful, and no one knows him here. But this is the home that Rose and her estranged husband have shared together, so he doesn't feel too great about that. They'll have to find another house in the area to live.

Emery hears movement inside the home and figures Rose must be awake. He reaches for the door handle, but Rose beats him to it from the other side. She pushes her way outside onto the balcony, her tousled hair covering her face. Emery can't help but smile.

"Morning," he says gleefully. "Did you sleep well?"

Rose ushers her way over to the railing. She nods with only a half-awake grin. "Is the jet lag hitting you?"

He shakes his head. "No, not yet."

Emery opens the blanket and invites her into his arms, setting down his latte on the railing before them to avoid spilling any. Rose almost leaps into his embrace, letting out a pleased sigh.

"I'm so happy you're home," she murmurs, burying her face in his chest.

Emery kisses her head as he snuggles her closer.

"About that..." he begins, and Rose quickly looks up at him. "Now that you're pregnant... umm..."

"Yes?" Rose presses, her brows furrowing.

"You know how my father was hounding me about taking over for him on the board and all that?"

"Yes?" She frowns.

"Well, he's going to expect us to move over there full-time. I just know him," Emery says, letting out an unpleasant sigh at the thought.

"You want to stay here?" Rose replies, voice soft.

"Yes." He nods. "I don't want to raise our child over there with all the noise that comes with being who I am. The role my father expects me to play is his essentially, and I don't want to do that."

"Well, what will happen then if you don't?" Rose gazes out at the horizon beyond the waves.

He hesitates, following her line of sight and blowing out a breath. "I don't know, I guess I will find out when I talk to him. I must tell my parents the news."

"Yes, of course. You should call them today."

"I will."

"What if we split our time between England and here? Would that work?" Rose suggests.

"You're not going to put up a fight to stay here full-time?" Emery asks, his jaw clenching.

"Not at all, I'm just saying… your father is as stubborn as you, and someone has to take his place, right?" She shrugs.

"What a nightmare this is going to be," Emery mutters.

"I'm sure your mom will support our choice to stay over here, right?"

He shakes his head, making a face. "I'm not sure. Even she thinks my father has a point. There is no one else they will accept to take over for the family business. Besides, it is a stipulation in the trust. It is set up that way, so our family retains control over our companies."

Rose rubs Emery's back as she kisses his chest comfortingly.

"We'll work something out. I mean, worst-case scenario, we split our time between both places, and we stay over there long enough for you to get settled. Then you can find someone who can run things while you take a step back partially?"

Emery shrugs, weighing her words. "Perhaps. But I just know they are also going to mention the fact that they are going to want to see their grandchild as much as possible."

Rose raises her brows. "That's understandable, if I'm being honest," she says.

Emery plans on telling his parents that he and Rose are expecting a baby in person rather than over the phone. They haven't visited Carmel yet, and he thinks it would be a wonderful idea. He hopes that with Rose being present when his father attempts to bring the subject up, it may deter his father from getting too pushy.

Rose has a choice after all, too. It's not just his life but hers, as well. It would be unfair to ask her to leave her life behind for him.

"I'm going to get it over with and call them right now," Emery says softly. The chilly morning air begins to pick up, blowing through their hair and making Rose shudder.

"Okay, let's go inside. It's too cold now; the clouds have hidden the sun," she expresses.

Emery follows her inside. He hasn't even spoken to his father yet and he already feels mentally drained. He reaches for his phone once inside and lets himself up to Rose's bedroom. Rose inserts more wood into the fireplace to keep the fire going. She sits in front of the flames snuggled up in the blanket Emery was using, his scent still lingering on it.

Truthfully, she never could have imagined things would pan out the way they have. Meeting Emery was something she never would have seen coming. She sensed something was afoot, but not necessarily a new man in her life.

Rose struggles to deal with the guilt she has for starting a relationship with Emery while still technically married, but things just happened so quickly and easily. Now that she has chosen Emery once and for all, she certainly feels as if a weight has been lifted off her shoulders.

Chapter 26

An hour later, Emery finally comes down the steps, his hair wet from a fresh shower.

"How did things go?" Rose asks eagerly.

"Good. I spoke to my mother, and I've invited them to come spend time with us here."

"Really?" she asks, her eyes widening in surprise.

"Yes, they are already on their way in fact. I didn't tell them that you're expecting. I figured that it would be best to tell them together, in person. What do you think?" Emery inquires.

"That's fine. I think it's better than telling them over the phone. It is more personal and special." She shrugs.

"Yeah, I agree." Emery nods, pulling her into a hug. "Although, I must admit my mother is psychic, so I can only assume she knows something."

Rose laughs. "Oh yes, for sure."

"She shares what she wants, I fear." Emery quips.

"Well, I bet she is instructed to. But also, I think she doesn't want to ruin moments like this by blurting it out to everyone."

Emery nods in agreement.

"Did you want to make breakfast here? Or do you want to go get brunch downtown?"

"I have to freshen up and get dressed first," Rose says, shrugging out of his hold. "I'll be quick!"

She runs up the steps to her bedroom as quickly as possible. Emery sits on the sofa awaiting her return. He peeks around at some of her photos on the fireplace mantel and sees that she still has photos of Phillip and herself up.

Emery can't help but feel that she's still struggling to let go of Phillip. It certainly doesn't help the situation, having the photos as a constant reminder. He struggles to not feel bothered by this. It is strange the way everything has come to pass, to see a love rival from the past return.

Emery reminisces when he first met Rose and how fateful it all felt. No matter how hard he tried, he would not have been able to stay away from her. The thought of them being together and growing a wonderful family is his ultimate idea of happiness and fulfillment.

Above all, he now understands why he was so restless prior to meeting Rose, why he fled home any chance he got. Sure, it was in part because he wanted to run away from his problems and responsibilities at home. But it also never felt comfortable being there. Now he knows it was Rose; she is his home personified.

Emery glances down at his feet, remembering how all his admirers wanted him but none of them made him feel the way Rose does so effortlessly. She is his vice, he admits.

As he sits in Rose's living room reflecting on himself, he acknowledges that he is a far cry from the rigidly righteous man he thought he was. Maybe he isn't so different now from who he used to be in the past... *Emmett James.*

Emery hears a creak on the steps and glances over. Rose comes down the steps hastily.

"I'm sorry, I tried to be as quick as possible," she says, a little out of breath.

He walks over to meet her at the door. "It's alright. Should we walk?" he suggests.

Rose shakes her head. "No, walking up that hill to downtown is exhausting. I'd be a sweaty mess by the time we get to the restaurant." She flashes him a grin.

Emery opens the door for her. "After you."

On their way to the restaurant, Rose sees Phillip walking down Main Street and into an art gallery. Rose is surprised to see him wandering about since work is pretty much his entire life. When together, he was so work obsessed that he hardly made time to go anywhere, at least until things became dire between them to the point of no return.

Emery spots him too; he gets a pit in his stomach at the sight. Once at their destination, Rose feels uneasy, worried that she may run into Phillip at brunch.

She communicates to the hostess that she would prefer to sit inside. Luckily there is room, and the woman obliges. As they are seated in a cute little booth by the window inside, Emery picks up on Rose's nervousness. She plays with the napkins and silver wear in front of her.

"What's wrong?" he inquires, brows furrowed in worry.

Rose shakes her head. "I don't know if I should talk about it." She shifts uncomfortably.

Emery takes his drink from their waiter and sets it down on the table. "Please do," he insists.

"Well, I didn't tell you. Phillip came over shortly before you arrived in town," Rose whispers. It is a small place, and the tables in the restaurant are quite close to one another. If she's not careful, anyone could overhear their conversation.

"He did?" Emery mutters back, annoyed. He twists his mouth to the side as he looks out of the window, shaking his head in disbelief. "He just won't quit, will he?"

"I told him I am pregnant."

Emery's piercing gaze zeroes in on Rose. "How did he take

the news?" he presses, his dark-haired brow raising ever so slightly as he awaits her answer.

Rose lets out an overwhelmed sigh as she recalls, "Not great. He got angry; he thinks you got me pregnant on purpose to keep me. He called you underhanded and deceitful."

Emery frowns, his eyes narrow as he hears that Phillip became hostile towards Rose and even more so because of her delicate condition. He laments not coming into town sooner.

"What else?" he asks, doing his best to control his anger as his jaw tightens.

"He was just angry, but he said he still wanted to be with me even if I am pregnant," Rose whispers.

As soon as he hears that, Emery sees red, his eyes narrowing into thin slits. But they are in public, so he reins in his knee-jerk reaction to what Rose is telling him. He fights the urge to find Phillip and beat him to a pulp.

"I... oh my God. I can't deal with this right now," he seethes, trying to calm himself down.

Emery knows he is being hypocritical; he and Rose didn't come together under the most pristine conditions. He is aware of that, but he would think that Phillip would give up already. Rose has chosen, and it isn't him.

"Do you prefer I change the subject? You asked." Rose grimaces.

"I am upset, but I would rather you tell me this," Emery mutters.

But before either of them can simmer down, a familiar voice cuts through the tension like a jagged knife.

"Hello, table for one please."

Rose immediately recognizes Phillip's voice. She sees him first before Emery, whose back is facing her husband. But by the look on her face, Emery can't help but notice something is horribly wrong. He follows her gaze to see what is so horrifying. The second he sees Phillip at the hostess stand, he rolls his eyes.

"Really?" Emery sneers.

"We need to go," Rose urges, preparing to get up.

But he shakes his head. "No, not yet. He's trying to make us uncomfortable; we will stay for a moment longer."

Phillip is seated a good distance away now, but it is awkward enough that he can see them from where he sits. He plays it cool and minds his business with the occasional glance over in their direction.

"I want to talk to him," Emery says to Rose, peering over at where her husband is.

"No, no, no," Rose whispers frantically. "No."

"Well, you need to finalize the divorce immediately. No time to waste now; you must cut that tie." His eyes narrow.

She nods, frowning down at the table. "I know. I will handle that tomorrow."

"Do you think he'd refuse to sign the divorce papers?" Emery asks.

Rose shrugs. "He hasn't given up on the relationship. I can only hope that eventually he realizes it's over."

After eating their meal, Rose and Emery finally get ready to leave. Emery glances over at Phillip when he sees him looking over at their table. He smirks and waves at him. Rose is mortified.

"Stop," she pleads. "Just stop."

Emery smiles innocently, raising his hands. "What? I'm being friendly."

Unable to take it anymore, Rose gets up from the table and walks out of the restaurant. Phillip watches her as she goes. His green eyes quickly glare at Emery as he lingers behind. Emery takes the opportunity to also pay Phillip's tab as he pays his.

Before leaving the restaurant, he waves again in Phillip's direction.

Rose walks quickly to the car, her face flushed in anger. Emery hurries to open her car door, but she slams it shut.

"Why did you have to do that?" she demands.

"Do what?! I just said hi. He was trying to make us uncomfortable, and I wasn't going to let him have it."

"You were trying to antagonize him!"

"Can we go? I'm not doing this out on the street," Emery insists. "Let's go." He opens Rose's car door again.

Reluctantly, she gets in, but not before Phillip approaches Emery from behind. Rose is sitting in the passenger seat mortified.

"I don't need your money," Phillip calls out, shoving several dollar bills at Emery when he spins around to face him.

"It was just a kind gesture," Emery lies.

"Sure, it was," Phillip says sarcastically. "You're not the type."

Emery raises his brow again with a scoff. "Excuse me?"

"You heard me," Phillip retorts hotly. "You're a piece of shit. You're really going to act like her being pregnant now wasn't intentional on your end?"

Emery's expression darkens even further. "Trust me, you don't want to do this here," he warns.

"Oh, I think I do," Phillip insists. He swings at Emery with everything he has.

"Stop!" Rose shouts as she steps out of the car.

"Get in the car!" Emery yells back at Rose from the ground, holding his face.

He scrambles to his feet and wipes away the blood from his lips.

"All right." Emery nods and swings back at Phillip.

He's been wanting to hit Phillip for quite some time now. As the men throw blows at each other, bystanders watch in horror. The hostess from the restaurant is told to call the police.

"Emery, please let's go!" Rose insists, as she audibly struggles for breath, eyes blinking rapidly.

It is a horrible sight to watch them fight each other. Phillip rains hits down on Emery with sheer hatred. In that moment, he unleashes all the pent-up anger he had not processed. Emery punches Phillip back, and at that point he's able to get Phillip off him.

Chapter 27

Rose takes Emery's arm and pulls him up towards her. "Let's go!" she shouts at him, her eyes darting between him and the growing crowd. "Enough!"

Phillip gets up and reluctantly stumbles away.

Emery gets in the passenger seat, in no condition to drive after what he just endured. Rose hurries back home, and by the time the cops arrive, all of them have gone.

The short drive home is quiet. Emery is bleeding, and his left eye is nearly swollen shut. As soon as they arrive back at the house, Emery insists on moving forward with selling the home and Rose finalizing her divorce as soon as possible.

Rose shakes her head in disbelief. "I don't want to talk to you right now! You are insane!"

"What?!" Emery exclaims. He stands by the fridge, helping himself to some ice for his eye. "You know it needs to be done."

"Why would you fight like that in the street? How embarrassing!" Rose yells in disgust.

"He punched me first. Are you kidding me?"

"No, you did something. Why did he practically throw money at you?"

"I paid for his tab. So what?" Emery challenges, resting the ice against his face.

"There it is." Rose scoffs. "You are trying to antagonize him."

"By paying his bill?" Emery retorts, narrowing his eyes.

Rose stares at him, not buying it.

"Go rest your face," she says angrily, darting up the stairs to her bedroom.

Still, Emery knows he was being petty and antagonistic, and he let Phillip's words get the best of him. But why is he only being blamed? After all, Phillip threw the first blow.

His injuries are starting to really hurt, and his parents are coming into town any moment now. They will inevitably ask about them, something he's not sure he wants to talk about.

Rose stays up in her bedroom for the rest of the afternoon. He gives her space before wandering upstairs. Emery lingers in front of the door for a moment apprehensively, he takes a deep breath and works up the courage to turn the doorknob. He keeps his head down and anticipates her rejection. Rose is lying in bed, watching a movie as he slowly approaches.

"Your mother just called me. She's at the airport and on her way here with your father," Rose says, not looking at him from where she's perched on the mattress.

Emery is surprised that his mother called Rose and not him. He assumes maybe she knows what happened earlier, he can only assume. At least until she arrives.

"What else did she say?" Emery inquires, drawing closer.

"Nothing much, just that she is on her way. Your father is very excited to be in town by the sound of his voice."

"Mmm..." Emery answers, biting his nails. He peers at her and back at the tv screen.

He lays beside her awkwardly. The ice has helped bring the inflammation down. Anxiously he peers over at Rose from where he rests, *swollen eye and all.*

"Are you only angry at me? Phillip did punch me first, you know… it's ridiculous." Emery frowns at the ceiling. "To think this is what I get for paying his tab? I was being generous!"

Rose rolls her eyes at him. "You were being petty," she retorts. "You knew what you were doing."

"Well, you know my parents are going to ask about my eye," he adds, trying to garner sympathy.

"Excellent! You can tell them yourself you instigated the fight!" she scoffs.

At around 4 p.m., Victoria and Sir Ashby arrive at Rose's home. She is beyond delighted to host them, although her home is far more modest than what the Williams are accustomed to, and that makes her a little nervous.

As soon as Rose opens the door for them, Victoria waves her hands in the air.

"Hello, darling. Where is he?" she groans.

"Uh, you mean Emery?" Rose stammers.

"Yes, where is he? Recovering from his injuries, I assume. Hiding away from embarrassment? If not, he should! Fighting out in the street, from what I saw! Emery!" Victoria shouts as she walks past Rose.

"Well, hello," Rose says hesitantly, greeting Sir Ashby as his wife breezes past. His gargantuan stature looks far larger in the front entrance of her cottage door.

"How are you?" he responds jovially.

"I've been better," Rose quips, her lips curling down slightly.

When Emery comes down the steps to greet his mother, he is still holding the ice bag to his face. His swollen lip is visible from where Rose stands at the door.

"Really?" Victoria exclaims, aghast as she takes in his appearance.

Emery shakes his head and rolls his eyes at her.

"You should be ashamed of yourself! You are dancing right on the line, you know that?"

"What?" Emery says, playing dumb as he averts his gaze.

"You know the guides *talk*; don't play stupid with me. This is strike two."

Rose stands behind her, taken aback by how angry Victoria is. It is frightening to see her quite this furious. Victoria usually has a very mellow disposition. But she doesn't blame Emery's mother, as the incident earlier was embarrassing.

"Your mother relayed to me what happened today," Sir Ashby confesses. "I would think that someone like you would show a little more decorum."

Emery bites his tongue.

"I have the guest bedroom ready for you two," Rose interjects, trying to ease the tension as she forces a smile.

"Are you sure? I don't want to be a burden! We booked a hotel," Victoria answers kindly.

"No! Why would you do that?" Emery says. "My home is just down the street; you can stay there."

"Oh, that will work," Sir Ashby replies, delighted.

Bidding farewell to Rose, Emery shows his parents to his home. He carries the luggage quickly through the door and hopes his parents like the place. It is the first time in a long time that he's hosted them in a space of his own.

"It really is right down the street," Sir Ashby notices, visibly pleased. "Very nice. We can walk on over once we are nice and rested."

"I need to meditate," Victoria hisses through her teeth to Emery, waving him off. "Off you go." She nods towards the door.

Victoria kicks her son out of his own home and slams the

door behind her. She knew he would be a struggle, but he incarnated back on earth to clear his karma. Not to add to it.

Emery is extremely unsettled that his mother is very upset with him. Their bond is incredibly close, and she has never raised her voice at him until now. He knows it must be serious...

He walks back to Rose's home after leaving his parents to rest at his place. He spots her through the window sitting by the fireplace, the glow of the flames casting an amber glow over her features. Seeing the door is unlocked, he lets himself in.

"You didn't lock the door?" Emery questions, shutting it behind him.

Rose turns her gaze to him. "Obviously not."

"You should've locked it! You never know," he scolds.

"Nothing ever happens here," Rose assures him.

"So, you're going to wait until something does?"

Rose sighs, refusing to look at him.

"I just want you to be safe," he insists.

Rose pats the empty spot on the rug beside her, inviting Emery to join her.

"When do you think we should tell your parents about the baby news? Do you think your mother knows already?" she says softly.

Emery shrugs. "I don't know. I didn't ask her."

"She obviously knew what happened earlier between you and Phillip."

He lets out a disgruntled sigh. "Yes, I know."

"Are they going to want to join us for dinner?"

Emery glowers into the fire. "I don't know, she's very upset, and I think they're tired. Maybe we can order something? I doubt they will want to go out."

"Okay." Rose shrugs as well.

Emery hugs her, bringing Rose's body closer to his. She rests her head on his shoulder while she watches the fireplace. Despite what has transpired earlier, she is excited to have Victoria in town; she truly enjoys spending time with her.

"I think if my mother doesn't already know about the baby, she is going to be thrilled," Emery remarks.

Rose smiles, chuckling softly to herself. "If she knows, she probably didn't want to ruin the moment with your stuff. She was angry!" She laughs. "You looked scared."

Emery flushes. "Well, she's never gotten mad at me like that before, and she was yelling at me in front of all of you!"

She only laughs harder.

"Stop!" Emery says with a smile, but then he flinches.

He brings his hand quickly to his lip, the smile causing the wound to reopen, eliciting pain.

Chapter 28

"I'm sorry," Rose says, noticing his discomfort with a frown. "Hold on."

She gets up from where she sits and disappears to fetch something to help. Rose comes back moments later with a cotton pad and an ointment for his lip.

"Here, this will help heal it quickly," she murmurs.

Emery stays as still as possible. His blue eyes watch her intently.

"What?" Rose asks, still fixated on his lip, aware that he is staring at her.

"I just like looking at you."

She smirks. "Should we order food now? And you can see if your parents want to join us?" she inquires. "I don't think they want to go to bed without eating."

Emery grabs his phone once she's finished. "I'll ask."

Once they agree to have dinner, Rose orders food from a local Italian restaurant. She takes it upon herself to set her table nicely the way Victoria did when she visited her in England. Rose knows her home is nowhere near as grand as Victoria's, but she hopes it will do. Emery's parents arrive just in time, about ten minutes after the food is delivered.

"Do you think we should tell them now?" Rose whispers to

Emery as they stand in the kitchen. His parents are now seated at the dining room table.

"Maybe," Emery murmurs back, keeping his voice low. "We will see how it goes; if she continues to be angry, then maybe another time."

Rose nods and carries the rest of the pasta in.

"I hope you will like this one," Rose remarks to Victoria with a kind smile. "It's my favorite choice from this place."

Victoria glances at it, pleased. "Oh, yes, I usually stick to the simple recipes. The classic red sauce. I can't tolerate the white sauce."

"I remember that. I think the only time you serve it is when Dad requests it," Emery joins in.

After everyone makes their plate, he clears his throat, grabbing his parents' attention. "Rose and I wanted to share news with you both."

Sir Ashby turns to look at his son, eyebrows raised. Even Victoria is leaning eagerly forward, waiting to hear what he has to say.

Emery takes Rose's hand as they sit down together at the table.

"We are expecting a baby," Emery says gleefully.

Victoria's eyes grow wide with excitement. Her hands come up to her mouth. "Oh! I must confess I already knew... I just didn't want to take this away from you."

Her hands fall away to reveal a tight smile. "I've been keeping it to myself." She elaborates further. "I've been bursting at the seams, trying to suppress my excitement!"

Sir Ashby smiles from ear to ear and pats Emery on the shoulder. He, too, is over the moon, delighted as can be. But it only lasts for a moment as he brings up the next obvious step in his mind.

"So, you'll move back home then, right?" Sir Ashby says. The room goes dead silent.

Emery's expression stiffens. He knew this was coming. "Father, not now."

Victoria gets up from her seat to hug Rose, clearing her throat. "I am so excited! Have you told anyone else?" she beams.

"A few people know." Rose replies.

The warmth that radiates from their embrace helps counter act the icy exchange between Emery and his father.

"We can have a discussion later on, just you and I," Sir Ashby says firmly to his son. Emery looks at his mother, brows pinched in annoyance.

"Yes, I can only assume what that may be about," he mutters back.

"I'm not going to get into it here and ruin this moment. But it is something that needs to be addressed," Sir Ashby insists, pointing his fork at his son.

"Stop," Victoria tells him, sitting back down and taking a sip of water.

Both Emery and Sir Ashby scowl at one another.

"Don't start locking horns already! We just got here," Victoria whines.

Rose sits there trying not to laugh; at this point, she's gotten used to their head butting the same way Emery's mom has. They do their best to enjoy their dinner together without the men ruining the mood.

"We were worried maybe you already knew about the pregnancy, and it wouldn't be much of a surprise," Rose admits to Victoria.

Emery's mother sets her fork down. "Yes, I did know." She nods. "But like I said I didn't want to take that away from you. What I see isn't always crystal clear. People fail to understand that our futures are filled with so many possibilities. The guides don't tell me *everything*. It takes away our ability to live in the moment and let some things play out the way they should. Does that make sense?"

Rose nods, taking a bite of pasta. "I was thinking we can spend some time together just you and me? I can show you around town and the beach here across the street."

Victoria raises her brows excitedly. "Oh, yes! That sounds great." She looks over at her husband, who is still locked in a scowl match with their son. "And you can use that time to talk with Emery, calmly!"

Emery glares at his mother. "Oh, so you're in on this too? Whose side are you on?"

"I'm playing both sides," Victoria says with a wink.

"Seriously?" he groans.

"No, but really. I'm going to have a grandbaby, and you mean to tell me I'm going to have to fly over here constantly to see you all? That makes me sad," Victoria confesses.

"Why not buy a home here?" Emery suggests. "You will love it."

She shrugs. "Oh, I don't know… I haven't been here long enough to see if I would like to live here."

"Well, the home could be just so you can be here with us comfortably when you visit. A place of your own? Part time…"

Victoria peers over at Sir Ashby, whose displeased expression says it all.

"I'm not going to get into it here, Emery," Sir Ashby says sternly. "You know you must move back home."

Emery throws his napkin down on the table, his lips tense in response to his father's words.

"We already agreed to not have this conversation now," he snaps.

Emery gets up from his seat and takes his plate with him. Rose also begins to clean up the table a little bit, since everyone is done eating. Victoria tries to do her share, but Rose immediately stops her.

"No, no, leave that there," Rose says, forcing a smile. "I've got it."

Chapter 29

Sir Ashby excuses himself back to Emery's home to smoke a cigar and unwind. Victoria stays behind for a little while longer, and Rose eventually joins her by the fireplace.

"Are you tired?" she asks Victoria.

"A little."

Emery comes to sit beside Rose and cuddles her into him.

"Why does he have to ruin everything?" he asks his mother glowering.

Victoria raises her brows and tightens her lips. "I know you're upset, Emery, but someone must take over for your father, and that someone is you."

Emery shakes his head, scoffing. "What's going to happen then? Have you thought of any alternatives? Why don't we just hire someone in my place to run it? I don't have to be there."

"You know, your father does not like the idea of bringing others into the company; they eventually start to make unauthorized changes. Besides, you know about the stipulation in the trust."

"Well, what if I just flew in for the important stuff?" Emery suggests. "And still live over here?"

Victoria sighs, glancing between him and Rose. "I don't think that would work. How will you know what's going on?"

"Conference calls?" he suggests.

"I don't know. Ask your father, but I would encourage you to maybe just stay in England for a month or two and get caught up with the way things are being run, and then maybe you can work from a distance?"

Emery agrees. "Now, if only dad were more reasonable."

"I'm not saying he will accept that, Emery. You know how he is. He's just as stubborn as you." Victoria shrugs.

Rose's body relaxes and sinks into Emery's arms, her eyes blinking slowly almost unable to open them again.

"Well, I'll get going then. I will see you all tomorrow," Victoria says to them both.

Emery gets up to walk his mother to his home. Rose hugs Victoria farewell and goes up to her room to get ready for bed. It's been quite a day.

Once outside, Victoria takes it upon herself to seize the moment and ask Emery something she has wanted to know since she found out about the pregnancy. "Was this pregnancy planned?"

"No," Emery answers as they begin walking home. "Why?"

"Because if it was… she didn't exactly choose you of her own free will. And you would have violated a very big universal law."

Emery turns to look at his mother pensively.

"That was the agreement—you were to let her choose on her own."

"She has!" he snaps. "I didn't do this on purpose, if that's what you're accusing me of."

"Did she? Did she choose you on her own? Or now that's she's pregnant, did she feel she had no choice but to choose you?" Victoria presses.

"What are you saying? You're thinking I did this on purpose to keep her?"

"I don't know what to think, but considering how badly you want her for yourself, I have to wonder whether you have done this on purpose. And it is my job to make sure you pass this test, Emery. That is my calling in both of your lives."

"We are passionately in love, and when caught up in the moment, we weren't exactly thinking about being careful. If that's what you want to know…"

"You must know that your guides will not be easy on you; if even one percent of you did this carelessly without ever considering that getting her pregnant would influence her choice in your favor, you have another thing coming."

Victoria walks up the steps to Emery's home once they arrive. Sir Ashby opens the door for her, and he extends his hand out to his wife, lovingly inviting her in. Before she enters, however, she turns to her son.

"There will be consequences, Emery." The gravity of what she relays to him is evident in her gaze. "And I won't be able to spare you from karma of your own doing."

"Wait," Emery says to her when she turns to go.

Victoria meets Emery where he stands.

"Do you really want to lock your soul further into this karmic loop you have imprisoned yourself in?" she asks her son. "Your insatiable love for her has always been your biggest strength but also your weakness."

Victoria pauses as she looks into her son's eyes.

"The lesson here is love. If you love someone, you do not strip them of their choice. You do not imprison them. You have failed in the past to let her choose; your former self killed the other man, and now… she's pregnant."

The fear in Emery grows. *Did I fuck up?* he thinks to himself.

"I didn't do this on purpose! It just happened," he insists.

Her eyes, now filled with sadness, peer back into his.

"Only time will tell. Like I said, there will be consequences. But now it is as if you're waiting for the other shoe to drop, if the guides find you in violation of the law."

Victoria walks up the steps to Sir Ashby.

"Goodnight," she says to Emery, vanishing inside.

His mother's words greatly affect him. He is terribly afraid that he may have messed up without meaning to. While walking back to Rose's home, his mind begins to overthink. *Did Rose really choose him wholeheartedly? Or is it because she's pregnant like his mother said and she felt she had no other choice?*

He must know for sure. When he arrives back at the house, he finds she is in the middle of a warm shower.

"Would you have still chosen me if you weren't pregnant?" Emery blurts out as he opens the shower door.

Rose turns in his direction and pushes the water out of her face, startled. "What?"

"Would you? I need to know."

Rose thinks for a moment. All Emery can hope for is that she says *yes*. Because otherwise it is clear that he violated the law of free will and choice, in this case, like his mother warned.

"I think I had already chosen you; I just wasn't being honest with myself. But the pregnancy just made it more obvious that you are the one that is meant for me." She shrugs.

Emery's expression appears as if all the blood has gone to his feet.

"So, the pregnancy influenced you further to choose me?"

"Well, yes." Rose affirms, lathering herself with soap. "What's wrong?"

Emery sits down outside of the shower, worried as his mother's words echo in his head.

"Do you want to join me?" Rose says, reaching out her hand to him. "Come join me."

Emery removes his clothes and enters the shower. He keeps

his distance at first, his widened eyes shift around lost in thought, his mouth runs dry.

"What happened?" she inquires, now concerned herself. The warm water falls on Emery's back. He looks into her eyes as he withholds what his mother told him just a few moments earlier. "Emery?"

He wraps his arms around her in a greedy fashion, basking in the suds that surround them both. "It's nothing," he lies.

His lips mesh with hers, igniting her flame of passion for him. Emery's hands hold Rose against the shower wall, and he presses his hips against hers, beginning to kiss her neck.

His fingers delicately stimulate her body before they enter her. Rose lets out a soft whimper, arousing him to no end.

His kisses grow in intensity, eager to devour her. Emery turns her around and slowly pushes his penis into her. Desperate for him, she stays put as he thrusts. Anchoring her further in his grasp, his left hand grips her hair as he tugs gently.

Rose pushes herself back into him, encouraging him to go into her harder.

"Don't hold back," she says breathlessly.

Emery shuts off the water and takes Rose out of the shower. Still soaking wet, he takes her on the bed. Rose moans louder while he enters her again.

Her hands grip his neck as he lies on top of her, water dripping from his face onto hers. Emery's demeanor changes, and he does with her as he wishes. His usual graceful moves in the bedroom have gone, and a more raw and dominant side of him emerges.

His kisses have turned into bites. His embrace has turned into feverish grips of lust. His oceanic gaze that was soft only for her is now simmering with hellish ardor.

His mouth engulfs her breast on its way to his favorite place—between her legs.

Emery's lips suck on her clitoris. She can't help but squirm beneath him from the pleasure. His hands firmly hold her in place, but the rapture is too intense, and Rose needs a break. She tries to squirm away from him, but he quickly pulls her back, denying her any respite.

Seizing the opportunity of her back facing him, Emery enters her from behind once more. His right hand grips her neck while he keeps Rose where he wants her.

He can feel she is almost there, and so is he. Emery loves to hear her say his name through her panting. He explosively finishes just before her; his hands stay on her hips while he releases himself from her body. Out of breath, he rests beside her.

Rose watches Emery, intoxicated by him. The bed is a mess, and the sheets need to be cleaned. They can't stay here. Emery takes the untouched blankets and guides Rose to the bedroom floor.

She sits on top of him naked, hungry for more. Her soft, lush lips kiss his neck. Emery's hands clasp on to her bottom, and Rose slowly works her way down.

She places him in her mouth. Emery weaves his fingers through her hair as he admires her. He doesn't last very long this time, and Rose finds herself a little disappointed.

While Emery spills all over the last of the clean blankets, she slumps over beside him. Panting, he sits up to collect his thoughts.

"How is this real? And we are expected to not be addicted to each other?" Emery says in disbelief. "Twice in a row... twice."

"You, twice in a row."

"I can't control it!" Emery insists, still trying to catch his breath.

"You can make it up to me another time," Rose quips.

Emery smirks, agreeing.

Chapter 30

The following morning, Emery and Rose are up early in the kitchen, making their morning coffee. He presses up against her as she waits for the machine to finish extracting the espresso.

Emery's hands grip her hips again. He buries his nose in her hair and neck, delighting in her scent. Rose pushes herself back into him, encouraging him to take her right then and there. The sleeve of her sundress cascades off her left shoulder, begging to be kissed.

Emery delivers a kiss or two before lifting her dress to gain access. Rose pulls down his bottoms, just enough to pull out her *"best friend."*

But this time, she isn't letting him dictate things. Rose guides Emery onto the kitchen floor and takes him there. Her knees will most likely bruise from the action, but she hasn't a care in the world. He owes her for last night.

Emery tries to fight for dominance, but when he sees Rose isn't letting up, he pulls down the top of her dress to expose her breasts; it isn't long before she climaxes without waiting for him. But as she does, he isn't far behind. He makes another mess on the kitchen floor.

"Be sure to clean that up before your parents arrive," Rose asserts breathlessly.

His mind still fogged by the pleasure, he watches her go back to the coffee machine to make their morning brews.

"I guess we are even now…" Emery says, panting.

"Yup." She grins.

Rose continues making both coffees as Emery cleans up.

"You think your parents are up yet?" she asks.

"Oh, for sure. They're probably waiting for me to call them. But if I don't call them, they will show up soon. I'm sure of it."

Rose pours the frothed milk into Emery's cup.

"What do you want to do today?" he asks Rose.

"I have to go finalize things with my divorce." She answers sobering the mood.

Emery alertly looks at her. "Today?"

"Yes, you told me I needed to sort this out, and I am. Today, everything is straight-forward; we signed a pre-nuptial agreement before we wed." Rose sips her latte.

"Will he be there?" Emery asks after a moment.

"Not today, but as soon as I do my part, I'm sure they will notify him of my actions, and he can respond accordingly."

Emery lets out a concerned groan.

"I'm staying optimistic." she says with a disinterested shrug.

"You think he really has resigned himself?"

"Given his actions, I don't think so. Why did you seem so shaken up last night?" Rose questions him.

Emery ponders if he should answer. His eyes focus on the frothed milk in his latte while Rose watches him, her brows furrowed in concern.

"Won't you tell me?" she presses.

"I don't think I should. That's the problem," Emery faintly responds.

"So, we are keeping things from one another?"

"Please don't do this…" he says, growing exasperated.

"No, *you* don't. What are you not telling me?" she demands.

Rose waves her hands in the air and moves her body away from Emery, feeling like he is turning his back on her by not telling her what is bothering him. He hasn't kept much from her before, and their psychological intimacy is something she cherishes. But this is as if a giant wall has gone up. She knows it will eat away at everything else unless he tells her.

"If you don't tell me, your mother will, and that will make this worse for you."

"Stop." He bristles.

"No, I won't. I want to know."

⚜

Emery isn't ready to talk to Rose about what his mother told him. The session Rose had with his mother really upset her, and now in her delicate condition, she should be shielded from certain information and treated with care.

But as they argue in the kitchen, a knock at the door interrupts them. Rose walks over to the door to see who it is, spotting Sir Ashby alone.

Rose swings the door open to greet him. "Hello."

He nods. "Good morning."

Emery waves at his father and for once is glad he is there to interrupt the ugly fight he and Rose were just about to get into.

"Come in, have a seat. Do you want some coffee?" Emery asks his father.

"Sure," Sir Ashby says, stepping inside the home.

Rose takes advantage of the fact that Emery's father is there. Knowing he won't be able to stop her, she darts up to her room and grabs her purse and comes down to leave quickly, trying not to speak to him.

"Where are you going?" Emery blurts in surprise.

"None of your business," Rose mutters.

He glares at her. "Rose!"

Sir Ashby sighs and makes himself comfortable over by the couch in the living area, preferring to stay out of the lovers' quarrel.

"Rose!" Emery calls out again. She ignores him as she gets in her car. "Where are you going?"

Without providing him an answer, Rose speeds off. Emery can only assume she isn't going to speak to his mother. Otherwise, she would've just walked down the street. Emery enters the home again, and his father glances over at him with a smile.

"What is going on?" he inquires, raising a brow.

Emery shakes his head. "She wants to know what mother told me last night."

A pensive look crosses Sir Ashby's face. "Oh, is it of a serious nature?" he asks.

"Do you still want that coffee?" Emery says, changing the subject.

Sir Ashby nods.

Emery walks to the kitchen to make him a latte.

"Simple, black coffee. Please."

"All right," Emery says after a brief pause. "Anyway, I just don't want to worry her. She's pregnant, and I don't want her stressing at all."

His father shrugs. "Your mother will most likely inform her if she asks her. You shouldn't keep things from one another."

"Oh, so Mum tells you everything?" Emery says sarcastically.

"Yes, I believe she does. We solve our problems together."

"Or does she make you think she tells you everything, but really doesn't," Emery presses.

Sir Ashby shakes his head. "Just be honest with her. It's best if it comes from you."

Emery brings the coffee over to his father and sits across from him. "Dad, this is more complex."

"Complex? What's more complex than being married to someone like your mother? She's a spiritually gifted goddess of a woman, and I'm a devoted catholic. You think we haven't had our quarrels?" His lips quirk into an amused smile.

"She didn't tell you?" Emery frowns.

"She tells me everything!" he insists, laughing. Sir Ashby proceeds to take a sip of his coffee.

Emery looks at his father in disbelief. But Sir Ashby, despite his jovial demeanor, is not joking.

"Your mother told me that you are to let Rose choose you of her own free will, and this pregnancy complicates things."

Emery's eyebrows raise, surprised to see that his father was in fact, not joking.

Sir Ashby looks back at his son with a smile. "I told you."

Emery sighs. "I didn't do this on purpose," he says to his father. "It just happened."

"Then you shouldn't worry about anything," Sir Ashby replies, but he watches his son as if waiting for a confession.

"But what if just the pregnancy alone is considered as me failing, just because it happened? She told me it did influence her decision." Emery stares at the floor, defeated.

Chapter 31

Rose is gone for a few hours. After her meeting with her divorce attorney, she opts to pick up Victoria if she is still at Emery's. She parks in front of his home and tries her luck. But there is no answer at the door, and as she walks back to her car, she sees Victoria over on the beach walking alone, glancing around investigating the area.

Not far from where she is, Rose runs over to her. She waves at her to get Victoria's attention. As she walks closer, Victoria finally sees Rose.

"You're here alone?" Rose asks her, catching her breath.

"Yes, Emery and Ashby are talking," she says sweetly.

Rose looks out to the horizon, taking in the sight of the pristine waves.

"Isn't it lovely?" Victoria says with a grin. "So, this is the beach I saw you at..."

"The beach you saw me at?" Rose inquires for clarification.

"Yes, before you and my son met, I received a vision of you sitting on this beach, sensing that your life was coming to a crossroads."

Rose turns to Victoria in astonishment, but she doesn't know what to say.

"You... you saw me? Before..." she struggles to express.

"Oh, yes," Victoria answers with a nod. "It is my job to see that you and Emery stay on course." She glances down at Rose's womb area. "But then again, I can only do so much; the rest is in your hands. There are certain things I can't foresee."

"Victoria, I wanted to talk to you about what you told Emery last night. He seemed worried."

She looks out to the ocean, doing her best to tame her own worries, but she is only human, after all.

"Yes, he should be if he's guilty. But I'm afraid it is more complicated than that now."

"What do you mean?" Rose asks, her lips curling into a frown.

Victoria stares at Rose then, her gaze piercing through her. "This choice is karmic, and it is yours alone to make. But you now being pregnant puts your choice into question. How much of it was your choice, and how much of it was Emery's?"

Rose thinks her words over, biting her lip.

"Would you have chosen him completely if you were not pregnant right now? Would you have committed to your choice?" Victoria presses.

"But I did already, in England. When we visited. I chose."

Victoria isn't so convinced.

"This choice must come from your heart, and I still sensed hesitancy in you. In committing to your choice one hundred percent."

Rose shakes her head. "But that doesn't mean I wouldn't have chosen him."

"You are not understanding… This pregnancy influenced you in your decision. That alone is enough to cause a problem with what the guides had made clear." Victoria pauses. "And you remember what you had seen in your session with me?"

Rose's breathing accelerates, unable to blink. "What are you saying? Is that the timeline we are on now?"

Victoria tries to calm her as best as she can. "We won't know until it comes to pass... it is hard to say."

"This is why he didn't want to tell me," Rose thinks aloud.

"He didn't want to worry you... or be honest." Emery's mother shrugs.

"What are you saying?"

"Were you actively trying to get pregnant?"

"No, we weren't trying at all. We just were intimate constantly. It was bound to happen." "Why do you ask, do you think Emery did this on purpose?" Rose asks.

"Only he can answer that," Victoria says, preferring to let Emery handle the situation. "Come on, let's go back. They must be wondering where we are."

Rose follows Victoria. When they arrive back at home, Emery and Sir Ashby look tense. But once Emery sees Rose, his face softens. He glances over at his mother, occasionally, concerned.

"Hey," Emery says, greeting Rose.

"Hi." Her reply comes a bit more stiff.

Emery hugs her and leans in for a kiss.

Rose kisses him back, but before he can pull away, she whispers in his ear. "We need to talk later."

He raises a brow and tilts his head in her direction.

"All right," he says back, reaching for another kiss.

Victoria sits beside her husband, greeting him with a serene smile. "The beach is lovely; we must go together later."

"Yes, it looks nice from here. It isn't too cold?" Sir Ashby remarks.

"No, dear, not at all."

He takes her hand in his and plants a kiss on it. "I think we should go take a nap. The time difference is getting to me."

Victoria agrees and follows his lead. "We will see you two

later," she says to the others before they head back to Emery's home.

They close the door behind them as they make their way out, leaving Rose and Emery alone to talk. As soon as the door closes, Rose pushes away from him. He doesn't chase after; he simply watches her as she moves around the kitchen and makes herself some tea.

"Your mother told me what she spoke to you about the other night," Rose begins.

"Oh," Emery says glancing over occasionally. He massages his hand to self-soothe.

"I want you to answer me honestly." She takes her tea to the sofa, where she seats herself. "Were you trying to get me pregnant?"

Emery sits beside her. "No," he answers firmly.

Rose stares at him, her expression stoic. "Are you being honest right now?"

"Yes, of course," he replies.

Chapter 32

"Why do I get the feeling that your own mother doesn't believe you?"

Emery doesn't have an answer for that.

"Why would she not believe you?" Rose presses further.

"I can only assume it is because she knows how bad I want you to myself and how scared I was that you may not have chosen me. But I swear, I wasn't actively trying."

"Well, let's hope that this doesn't count as you trying to bypass karma in some way. Even if you didn't do this on purpose," Rose sighs.

Emery pushes his hand through his hair.

"Yeah, I know. But that is what my mother was talking about when she brought it up the other night, and to make matters worse, you are admitting that it did influence your decision. Even if not completely."

"That is where you're sort of wrong."

"How so?" His gaze flits over to her.

"Because I can still choose myself. I can raise this baby alone. I didn't have to choose you, but I did because I love you. You are the man I need and want."

Rose holds Emery's hand.

"You're far from perfect and don't always win against your darker impulses. But I love you unconditionally."

Emery smirks. "Lucky me."

Rose smiles. But then her thoughts drift to her divorce and her time with Phillip. That chapter is ending, and there is no going back now.

"I think we should start looking at a new home," Rose says, tearing up.

"What's wrong?" Emery asks, frowning in concern.

"I just love this place, but it doesn't make sense to keep it now."

"Well, if Phillip agrees to let you have it, you can just keep it on your real estate portfolio," Emery suggests.

"It's deeper than that; it's what the home signifies to me. Keeping it would be like still having a piece of the past lingering around. It doesn't feel right to me."

"Oh, I see," Emery sighs.

The home has meant so much to Rose; she loves the area and how close it is to the beach. She will miss her night strolls and the early morning walks, too.

But it is also sentimental because it is her saying goodbye to Phillip.

It is odd, to feel the pain that she does. She is not in love with him the way she is with Emery. Her love for Emery is different; it is deeper, all-consuming.

Her love with Phillip was calm but distant, as if there was a wall between them, a wall only she was able to detect once Emery showed her true emotional depth. Emery showed her what it feels like to become one with another, to merge so completely, embracing one another's dark and light. Emery has shown Rose that unconditional love means loving both with equal measure.

Love is not always soft and light. Love can also be dark, twisted, and imperfect. Tough yet gentle, deep, and passionate. It is to be felt with all of one's soul.

Emery has loved her so completely, and he is utterly unapologetic about it.

He has awakened in her a desire to experience this deep, cathartic love fully. Having only half loved is equal to living in a desolate wasteland, never having tasted water.

Rose prepares mentally for when she will have to say her last goodbye to Phillip.

But it must be done.

❦

The following morning, Rose's divorce attorney emails Rose to notify her that Phillip has agreed to swiftly sign his part of the paperwork. Upon reading the email, she is pleased with the outcome.

But the lawyer lets her know that Phillip wants to be there to discuss the home she currently resides in. Rose can only assume that maybe he wants to keep it. She agrees to meet and asks Emery to stay behind. He respects her request and goes to see homes with his parents in the area to get a feel for what is currently on the market.

When Rose arrives at the meeting, she is extremely nervous but tries to hide it. Upon seeing Phillip, she sees he still has injuries to his face; it pains her to see him that way.

Phillip and his lawyer make it clear that Rose can keep the home. The meeting only takes about ten minutes. Rose signs her share and Phillip his.

"Is this all?" Rose asks when they're done.

"Yes," her lawyer says. "Everything is finished. All that's left is to file the paperwork."

"Okay, thank you," she replies, leaving abruptly.

Phillip follows her out.

"Rose, can I talk to you for a moment?" he asks as they

stand outside. "I wish you the best, truly. I'm sorry I couldn't be there for you."

Rose struggles to look at him. "I'm surprised you signed the papers so quickly."

Phillip's emerald-green eyes soften, and he shakes his head in disappointment. "I had to. I love you."

"What are you talking—" "When you love someone, you let them go," Phillip says earnestly. "And despite everything, I love you. I mean that."

He looks at her, teary-eyed.

"I'm sorry I prioritized work and money over you. The truth is, I just never felt like I was enough for you. I thought that maybe if I had a lot of money, then the feeling would go away... but it never seemed like enough. Until it was too late."

The patterns of the past all hit her at once along with the realization that Phillip's feelings are, in fact, Pierre's lingering memories in his soul.

A tear falls from Rose's eye as she watches him leave, defeated. She is irrevocably astounded by the connection she has made in that moment. As if the past has come full circle, she realizes then that no matter what happens, she always ends up with Emery. Even if she tried to the point of exhaustion, it would never work with Phillip.

The realization breaks her heart into a million pieces. Yet, she must keep moving forward.

Chapter 33

When Rose drives up to her house, she quickly rushes in to find that no one is there. She figures she can pull herself together before Emery and his parents get back.

She sits in her room and doodles in her journal, hoping the evidence of her tears fades away as the minutes tick by. She knows leaving Phillip behind in her past is the right thing to do, but she is still puzzled by her emotions. She fails to understand herself.

Rose ends up taking a nap after doodling. The heavy weight of releasing her grief leaves her depleted. Emery and his parents arrive back just before dinnertime. Emery enters her bedroom and sees her fast asleep.

He quietly lies next to her, pressing his nose into her neck to sniff her affectionately.

"Wake up," he whispers. "Wake up, baby."

Rose opens her eyes a little. Upon seeing him, she closes them once more.

"Do you want to go to dinner?" he asks.

But Rose is in no mood to go out; her eyes are puffy, and the swollenness from crying earlier hasn't gone away. She buries her face in her pillow, hoping he won't notice. He pulls her towards him and cuddles her in his arms.

"Are you okay?" he inquires with his deep, velvety voice. "How did things go?"

Rose begins to cry some more; she covers her eyes with her hands.

Emery holds her tighter. He knows how much it pains her and how difficult things are. But he's glad at least things were dealt with. It had to be done, and the longer she procrastinated, the more painful it would be. Now that she is pregnant, the pressure is on to close that chapter and move on.

"I love you," Emery tells her, doing his best to soothe her.

She hugs him and rests her head on his chest. "My eyes are too puffy to go out," Rose protests.

"Well, I can bring you something here?"

She shrugs. "Yeah, I guess."

Emery kisses her head. "What do you want?" he asks.

"I'm not sure. I'm not that hungry, so I don't want a big meal."

"So perhaps a salad?" Emery suggests.

"Perhaps not," Rose quips. She smirks and sits up, wiping her cheeks. "I think maybe a soup would be good for this cold weather."

Emery admires her as she sits before him; he will forever worship at her feet. She isn't even aware of how much power and influence she has over him—mind, body, and soul. He wants to be consumed by her every day of his life, and even then, that wouldn't be enough.

"What?" Rose asks. She covers her eyes again, embarrassed by how puffy they are.

"I just love you," he answers simply. "I would admire you all day if I could."

Someone knocks at the door. "Emery?" Victoria calls from the other side.

Emery quickly gets up to walk to the door. He steps out in the hallway to speak to his mother and give Rose some privacy.

"Are we going to dinner?" Victoria inquires. "I'm a bit hungry now, and so is your father."

"Okay, we can go. Rose is staying behind, but I need to bring her food."

"Oh, is she okay?" Victoria asks. She places her hand delicately over her mouth, her eyes flicker at Emery awaiting an answer.

"She's not feeling well, she needs time."

Victoria nods. "Alright, well, we'll be waiting downstairs."

Emery enters the room again to let Rose know they are leaving.

"I'm going to take a bath," she says, nodding goodbye. "Have a good time at dinner."

Emery sighs, wishing he could stay with her. He plans to grab food for Rose and himself and come straight back. He lets his mother know that he won't be staying with them for dinner.

Sir Ashby takes it upon himself to pick his top choice then, instead of accommodating Emery's selected restaurant. When Emery does return thirty minutes later with food, Rose is in the bath enjoying the warm water alone. She hears the door of her bedroom open and sits up alarmed, but once she sees Emery with the bags of food in his hand, she smiles.

He sets up the food on trays for both of them and prepares to join her in the water.

"You left your parents at dinner?" Rose asks in surprise.

"Yeah, they're fine. I told them I was coming back to stay with you."

Emery undresses bit by bit. Rose watches with a devilish smile as he dips his leg in the water, making room for him in the tub. Rose positions herself on top of his body and leans in for a kiss.

"Are you feeling better?" Emery hums.

"A little," Rose answers with a sigh. "Today was tough. But he gave me this house," she adds.

Emery's brows raise upon hearing the news. "He did?"

Rose nods and plays with the water a little bit with her hand, swishing it around, watching the ripples form. She remembers what Phillip told her earlier and how he admitted to her that he never felt like he was enough for her, and her heart hurts once more.

"What do you want to do with the house?" Emery asks pensively.

Rose lets out an overwhelmed sigh.

"I love this house so much, but it is too painful to keep it. I feel it has so many memories stored here." She shrugs.

"I saw some beautiful homes today, with large yards and a lot of privacy. They're in a different area. So, it isn't right off the scenic drive. But the one I liked the most isn't too far from here."

Rose glances up at him. "Were there any here? In this neighborhood?"

"Yes, one right around the block from here. It is bigger and it has unobstructed views of the ocean," Emery replies. "I have some of the listings, and I can show them to you later if you'd like?"

"Yes! I want to see," she answers curiously.

After about thirty minutes in the water, Emery's hands caress Rose's curves, in hopes of enticing her. He enjoys the sensation of her soft skin. His lips delightfully meet hers. Emery can sense she is enchanted; her fixed gaze encourages him to proceed.

She eagerly reciprocates, her fingers enmeshing in his dark, thick hair. Her lips devour his as his hand clutches her breast.

"I think we should move to the bed," Emery suggests huskily.

Rose lets him carry her to the bed, and she laughs as they are both still covered in bubbles. Emery's fingers stroke and stimulate her. He presses his fingers inside of her, and Rose lets out a soft murmur.

Watching her disheveled in all her sensual glory in his clutches is devilishly satisfying to his soul. Emery positions her just how he wants her and lets himself in.

Rose's flushed cheeks exude an ethereal glow, and her hands grip his shoulders while the pleasure he provides overwhelms her senses. She closes her eyes as her soft moans increase, driving Emery wild.

He bites her neck and thrusts harder. His hand grips Rose's leg to secure her in place. Her nails dig into his skin, and the rush of pleasure she experiences in that moment makes her feel as if she is ever so slightly hovering above her body.

Chapter 34

Emery's parents go for a walk on the beach together after dinner, hand in hand. Victoria admires and explores Carmel's beach as if it were a historic sight. To her, it feels that way, at least. Many of her visions that she received of Rose were when she was at that exact beach.

She feels guided to a specific spot as spirit shows her the apparition Rose had seen early on in her awakening. She is told that Rose thought it was just a dream, but it wasn't. It was the Angel of Death Azrael appearing before Rose to warn her of what was to come.

One part of her life was ending, and another was beginning, and this energy is around her, helping her deal with the pain of the transition.

Many fear this angel because he is also referred to as *the Grim Reaper.*

Although, it is clear he appeared to her as a bright light over the beach to avoid frightening her further. It is clear to Victoria why he appeared; his energy makes the most sense to aid her during this time.

Death, as they say, is but an illusion or just another word for transformation. As we change, we shed who we once were to allow the new to emerge. Both cannot reside together.

Victoria sits down on the sand with Sir Ashby.

"This place is enchanting, don't you think?" she says to him.

"It is," he beams, allowing himself to sink into the soft sand beneath him. He reaches into the breast pocket of his blazer and pulls out a cigar and cutter.

"Oh, here we go," Victoria sighs, growing sullen.

"What? It's a special occasion! We are going to be grandparents!" he exclaims.

Victoria looks around cautiously. "I don't think you can smoke here."

"It's fine! No one is out here!" Sir Ashby assures her; he lights up and enjoys his cigar with the beautiful view before them. "I can see why he likes it here," he remarks to his wife after a few puffs. "No one knows us here, no one bothers us. It's quiet."

"Yes, it's very peaceful, and the homes look like cottages from a fairy tale!" Victoria replies, delighted. "They are incredibly charming!"

"Should we buy one?" Sir Ashby suggests. "The couple will be here a lot, I know this. Emery isn't going to move to England full-time. He will split his time between here and with us."

Victoria turns to look at her husband, surprised that he gave in. She can't help but ponder as to why.

"He wouldn't cave," Sir Ashby says with a sigh. "And I want to see my grandchild and be a part of their life as much as possible."

"Did he threaten to keep the baby from you if you did not concede?"

"Not outright, but I fear that is where things would go if I didn't let him get his way."

Victoria listens to him as he reveals more.

"Emery expecting a child now changes things. It isn't just

him, and I won't lose my grandbaby before I've even known the child. He has, in a way, leverage over me now, I hate to admit."

"So, you want to buy a home here?" Victoria asks.

Her husband nods. He taps the ashes away from his cigar before responding, "It seems like the next natural step, and since we are here, we could use this time to look around ourselves."

Victoria closes her cardigan as the wind picks up around them.

"Peaceful anonymity is another good reason to move here. I have really grown to like Carmel in the short time we've been here." She adds.

Sir Ashby puffs his cigar and blows out the smoke into the air. A pensive look appears on his face as he admires the ocean water crashing onto the shore.

"He's madly in love with Rose," he says, taking another hit of his cigar. "He's different because of her; have you noticed?"

Victoria agrees wholeheartedly. "Yes, I have."

"He's passionate and ferociously protective of her. I have never seen anything like it. His usual temperament is calm, collected," Sir Ashby says with a short pause as he thinks his words over. "Aloof, in his own little world. And this version of him is deep, passionate, and sometimes a little dark…"

"That's what happens when you meet *the one*, is it not?" his wife quips.

Sir Ashby chuckles. "Sure, but he's downright obsessed with her. The way he watches her, the attentiveness… one can't help but notice it."

"Their souls have a lot of history together. When one has that much karma with someone, it isn't going to be light and fluffy!" Victoria reminds him.

Sir Ashby sighs as he finishes up his cigar.

"Well, I wish them all the best. Are they planning the

wedding yet, or are they going to wait since she is expecting now? Has she told you anything?"

"I think they are going to elope." Victoria shrugs.

"Did Emery tell you that?"

"No, it's what I have seen," she confesses. "But that can change."

Sir Ashby raises his brows. "I'd like a wedding," he says with a laugh.

Victoria shakes her head at him. "It's not for you to decide these things."

"I know, but I'm just stating what I'd like. Get everyone together. Friends, family."

Victoria rolls her eyes. "After what happened at the engagement party?" she scoffs.

"That was downright ridiculous!" Sir Ashby recalls the moment angrily. "The Montgomerys should be ashamed of themselves."

"It wasn't Jack. He had nothing to do with it," Victoria says in his defense.

"It doesn't matter if we do have a wedding; they will not be invited. I felt bad for Rose that night, you know… I didn't want her to leave," Sir Ashby continues.

Victoria's lips thin as she recalls what happened.

"I didn't either, but she didn't feel comfortable staying any longer; that's what she told Emery, anyway."

Sir Ashby lets out an exasperated sigh. "He was devasted when she left. Absolutely inconsolable."

Victoria did her best that day to try and assist Emery, but there was nothing she could do. The Montgomerys had briefly gotten what they wanted, and there was a part of her that feared Rose would make a different choice. But now that her choice is sealed, the question remains; *was the law of free will violated by the pregnancy?*

Even if Emery wasn't seeking to get her pregnant, it's the one thing she is afraid of; the consequences will be heavy, that's for sure.

"Shall we head back to Emery's, love?" Sir Ashby suggests.

Victoria smiles. His suggestion snaps her out of her mind and back into the moment.

"Yes, let's head back. I'd like a nice cup of tea."

Sir Ashby and Victoria decide to extend their stay in Carmel for several months. Refusing to miss any milestones of Rose's pregnancy they put their plan in motion to be nearby. They purchase their own property close to Emery and Rose's new home, as Rose's baby bump grows, Emery and his family all take turns doting on her, hand and foot. To avoid uprooting Rose any further, they all decided together that it would be best that Rose remain in Carmel until the baby is born. The process of moving homes in her delicate condition was stressful enough. Back in England, Nannie is left in charge of taking care of the William's estate until Victoria and her husband return.

Rose finally gets around to breaking the news to her family despite the whirlwind of events unfolding in her life. Hand in hand with Emery during a quiet lunch in Big Sur she dropped the enormous life update on her parents. She knew it would be a massive shock to them since everything unfolded very quickly, but she felt it was important for them to know. The meeting did not go as smoothly as she had planned. Rose's conservative parents now refuse to speak to her, they rose from their seats mid-lunch upset about the whole thing. Leaving Emery and Rose devastated. All they could do now, is hope that they come around, eventually.

Chapter 35

9 MONTHS LATER

R ose catches her breath while moving about the kitchen. She has been nesting peacefully in her new home. Everything is to her liking, although it was hard saying goodbye to her former residence. She is happy to be past that now. Emery and his family have been lovely, assisting her with anything she needs. It can be a little much sometimes, they fuss over the smallest things. She likes being independent and doing things for herself, but they insist on not letting her lift a finger. Rose is having Victoria over for lunch today. They've established a nice little routine; the women have their time together apart from Emery and his father. Victoria is teaching Rose how to tap into her intuition through meditation. In hopes that one day she will reach her level of mastery. Emery makes it difficult for Victoria and Rose to have their time alone, he is clingy and has weaseled his way into their lunches on several occasions. It isn't just him though, at times Sir Ashby invites himself too, assuming it's fair game if Emery is there.

Rose sets the table with the fine China Emery gifted her not too long ago.

"Let me do it." Emery asserts.

A very winded Rose reluctantly allows him to take over.

"Your mother will be here any minute. Are you going golfing with your dad?" she inquires doing her best to be discreet. She doesn't want to hurt Emery's feelings at all, but he wants to be attached at the hip. While Emery sets the table, he drops his head and begins to sulk.

"No, not today." He answers, disappointed that Rose isn't inviting him to stay.

Suddenly the doorbell rings. His parents are at the door, Rose waddles over and swings the door open. She is surprised to see Sir Ashby in tow, it looks as if both men have planned to join them.

"He came with." Victoria mutters before saying hello, twisting her mouth, she scrunches her nose and shoots a look over at her husband. Rose smiles and sighs.

"Well, I guess he can stay." She says softly. Emery perks up from where he stands, still setting up the table. If Sir Ashby can stay, that means he too can join them.

"What are we having today?" Victoria asks. "Pasta?"

"No, Filet mignon. I've ordered from a new restaurant in town." Rose says. "I hope you don't mind; I know it's more of a dinner choice."

Victoria shakes her head and takes a seat at the table.

"Don't worry about me, I'm fine with it." she responds delighted.

Rose picks up her glass of water and takes a sip.

"It's getting harder for me to breathe." She quips. Affectionately rubbing her bump.

Victoria's eyes widen. "Oh, I bet."

"So, you both really are waiting to find out the gender of the baby?" Sir Ashby asks. He sits beside his wife like a contented child. Pleased that he got his way and was able to join them.

"Yes! It adds to the excitement!" Emery adds. His lip's part forming a gleeful smile.

His father shakes his head.

"I want to know. How am I supposed to know what clothes to buy my grandchild?" he whines.

Victoria rolls her eyes.

"Oh, please! Stop. You'll know once the baby is born, and you can do the shopping then."

Sir Ashby takes his plate from Emery.

"Well, I guess no lesson today." Victoria sighs. "Have you been meditating like I told you?"

Rose nods.

"Right at five a.m. like you told me."

"It's best, you can enter a deeper meditation that way. Other times your brain may be too active. It takes longer to quiet the mind." Victoria claims.

Rose has been learning very quickly from Emery's mother, although quieting her mind in the beginning was rough. The meditations in the morning like Victoria has suggested have granted her a breakthrough.

Both Emery and Rose take their seats at the table. Emery places an affectionate hand on Rose's stomach.

"So…" Victoria says. "What do you think you are having? Boy or girl?"

Rose turns to Emery before answering.

"You want to say first?" she asks him. A mischievous grin forms on her face. Emery finishes chewing his food before answering, Victoria's blue eyes focus on her son.

"I think… a boy." Emery guesses.

"I think, I'm having a little girl." Rose says confidently.

"I have to say my guess is a little girl too." Sir Ashby chimes in smiling excitedly. He can't wait to meet his grandchild. If the baby is a girl, she will have both Emery and his father wrapped around her little finger.

"What about you, Victoria? What's your guess?" Rose asks she raises an inquisitive brow. "Or the better question is.... do you know already?" She rests her elbows on the table and leans forward.

Victoria shakes her head she covers her mouth to stop a smile from forming.

"Don't do this to me!" she says laughing.

The entire table now, has their sights fixed on her. But in that moment a gushing sound suddenly takes them all by surprise. Everyone's eyes widen. Rose rises from her seat with a gasp.

"Oh, my goodness!" she exclaims frantically. "It's me!"

The realization of Rose's water breaking prompts everyone to rise from their seats immediately. Victoria assists Rose to the car while Emery rushes to the nursery room to fetch the hospital bag.

"Well, the moment of truth is upon us." Sir Ashby beams. "We will see who's guess is right."

Acknowledgements

I would like to kindly thank everyone who assisted in bringing this wonderful book to life. Thank you to the team, Sam, Bryn, and Ashley for your wonderful work. To my family for their incredible support and patience. I am beyond grateful.

www.ingramcontent.com/pod-product-compliance
Lightning Source LLC
Chambersburg PA
CBHW020839260626
47169CB00003B/1062